PRAISE FOR THE MYSTERIES OF TAYLOR McCAFFERTY

"This down-home–style whodunit is a lot of fun. . . . McCafferty's characters are amusing and her story is fast-moving and entertaining."

—*West Coast Review of Books*

"McCafferty writes skillfully. Blevins' narrative voice is convincing."

—*Publishers Weekly*

"A wonderful series."

—*Mystery Lovers Bookshop News*

"Witty and satisfying and smart. . . . McCafferty's plot is clearly clever, but her writing is what clicks with the reader."

—*Lexington Herald-Leader* (KY)

"A solid example of soft-boiled P.I. writing. . . . A novel of small-town manners that succeeds because of its use of humor."

—*Mystery News*

Books by Taylor McCafferty

Pet Peeves
Ruffled Feathers
Bed Bugs
Hanky Panky
Funny Money

Published by POCKET BOOKS

FUNNY MONEY

A HASKELL BLEVINS MYSTERY

Taylor McCafferty

POCKET **STAR** BOOKS
New York London Toronto Sydney Singapore

This book is a work of fiction. Names, characters, places and incidents are products of the author's imagination or are used fictitiously. Any resemblance to actual events or locales or persons, living or dead, is entirely co-incidental.

An *Original* Publication of POCKET BOOKS

A Pocket Star Book published by
POCKET BOOKS, a division of Simon & Schuster Inc.
1230 Avenue of the Americas, New York, NY 10020

ISBN: 0-671-00129-9

First Pocket Books printing March 2000

10 9 8 7 6 5 4 3 2 1

POCKET STAR BOOKS and colophon are registered trademarks of Simon & Schuster Inc.

Cover by John Zielinski

Printed in the U.S.A.

To
Annalise and Stephanie Reusche,
who are more fun
than the entire population of Pigeon Fork

ACKNOWLEDGMENTS

The author wishes to thank her daughter-in-law, Paula King, for the use of her cat, Kiefer, as a model for the cat, Goliath, in *Funny Money*. I do want to make it clear that Goliath's personality differs from Kiefer's completely. Even though Kiefer is every bit as large as Goliath, sweet Kiefer doesn't seem to know how to throw his weight around.

I also want to thank my twin sister, Beverly Taylor Herald, for acting as my first reader. It's a good thing that she and I write another series together, or I'd feel doubly guilty for taking advantage of her.

And finally, I want to thank Robert Reusche for all the ways he helped me when I was finishing this book. I would list them all, but I'd embarrass both of us.

FUNNY MONEY

1
§

Private eyes and preachers have a lot in common. I might not have thought so a few months ago, but nowadays, after everything that's happened, I know that it's true.

Folks tell both private eyes and preachers the kind of secrets they wouldn't even think of telling anybody else. Folks turn to both of us for help only when they're in big trouble—and even then, usually as a last resort. *And* folks often seem to expect both of us to work miracles.

Of course, none of this came to mind on that cold, dreary Wednesday in February when Brother Tallman, the preacher over at the Pentecostal Church of the Holy Scriptures on Highway 60, walked up to me in my brother Elmo's drugstore. All I realized at that particular moment was that Brother Tallman was interrupting me, and I was busy. As the only private eye in the bustling metropolis of Pigeon Fork, Kentucky, I was working on a real big case.

A real big case of women's deodorant.

I was working on emptying out the case and restocking the shelves in the women's toiletries aisle. I was also cursing out my brother under my breath. "Damn you, Elmo Blevins, damn you, damn you, damn you."

I know this doesn't sound all that brotherly of me, but I had good cause. It had just dawned on me, as I was reaching into the carton for yet another Ban roll-on in the country fresh scent, that it had been exactly two years to the day that Elmo had made me an offer I couldn't refuse.

Elmo had offered to let me have the office over his drugstore totally rent-free. The only stipulation had been that I'd agree to help out in the store during my slow times. It hadn't even occurred to me back then to wonder why Elmo was suddenly being so all-fired generous, especially considering the fact that Elmo had not exactly been leaping for joy at the prospect of my finally doing what I'd always dreamed of—opening up my own private detective business. In fact, ever since I'd moved back to town, Elmo had been pestering me to join him in what he often referred to as "the exciting world of drugstore management."

Of course, back then I'd been under the impression that Elmo understood English. This, I now realize, had been my first mistake. Having said again and again quite clearly that drugstores did not figure prominently in my plans for the future, I'd just assumed that the subject of my drugstore career was pretty much closed. In fact, far from putting two and two together, right after Elmo had made me his offer, I'd practically fallen all over myself, thanking him and telling him how much I appreciated his generosity.

As Elmo himself used to say when we were kids, mimicking Bugs Bunny right after Bugs made Elmer Fudd look like an idiot for the millionth time: What a maroon.

I hate to say it, but I was a maroon, all right. My only excuse was that I'd been working homicide in Louisville for the eight years immediately preceding this particular chat with Elmo. I reckon I'd clean forgotten just how slow a town the size of Pigeon Fork could be. Let me tell you, with a total population of 1,511, Pigeon Fork is not exactly your hotbed of criminal activity. In fact, on some days, Pigeon Fork doesn't seem to have any activity at all, criminal or otherwise.

All this could possibly explain why in the last six months the only kind of cases I'd worked on were the cardboard kind, much like the one right in front of me.

There was also something else that could

possibly explain it. I suppose, if I were to be brutally honest, I'd have to say that I don't exactly fit your typical private eye mold. When folks start thinking about hiring themselves a private detective, they pretty much have in mind somebody who looks like Magnum P.I. Or maybe Paul Drake, that suave, handsome guy who did all the detective work for Perry Mason on the old classic TV show. I can't say I resemble either one of those private eye types. I have been told more than once that I do resemble a television star, however. Unfortunately, the star everybody always seems to have in mind is not exactly suave, and not terribly handsome either—it's Howdy Doody.

Can you believe folks actually said this to my face? Frankly, I always hoped that the folks who told me this were just being cruel, and that Howdy and I really don't have all that much in common. It does depress me, though, to have to admit that Howdy and I do both have red hair. And we both wear checked shirts and blue jeans quite a bit. And, yes, between Howdy and me, we have enough freckles to spatter the entire population of Rhode Island.

So, OK, I reckon it is possible that the Howdy Doody issue might've contributed a tad to how slow my business had been over the last few months.

Mostly, however, I think business was slow because Pigeon Fork was slow. A thing I do believe Elmo had to be extremely aware of long before he made me his so-called generous offer. "Damn you, Elmo," I muttered again under my breath, lining up the Ban roll-ons on the middle shelf so that all their labels faced out, "you got me to come into the drugstore business whether I liked it or not. Damn you, Elmo, damn—"

"Brother Blevins?"

I immediately stiffened. I knew, of course, without even turning around exactly who had spoken. For one thing, the voice was pretty distinctive. It's real deep, real loud, and it always seems to be quavering some. So that every word vibrates with emotion. With a voice like that, you could make reading the phone book sound like a sermon.

For another thing, there aren't too many folks in town who call me Brother Blevins. Hell, even Elmo doesn't call me that, and he really is my brother. Nope, the only folks around these parts who address everybody they see as Brother Somebody and Sister Somebody Else are folks who are members of the Pentecostal Church of the Holy Scriptures.

I got to my feet and turned to face my visitor. Sure enough, it was Brother Isaac Tallman, minister of the aforementioned church. The reverend was in his late forties, so he was only about a dozen years older than me, and yet he always seemed a lot older. I reckon it was on account of his giving sermons and all. Anybody who has figured out what's what so well that he can lecture other people on it, well, he has got to be a lot older than me.

For a man with a name like Tallman, he was only about five feet, eight inches tall. The way I figured it, this was no doubt one of the reasons he'd gone into the ministry. As a short kid called Tallman, he'd probably been teased and ridiculed in school on a daily basis from kindergarten on. Having done the whole martyrdom thing as a child, I reckon he decided it just naturally followed that he would be a preacher.

Today the reverend was wearing his usual: a black shirt, black slacks, black boots, and a black suit coat. On more than one occasion I'd heard Brother Tallman go on and on about the evils of country music. I'd never quite had the heart to tell him that he dresses just like Johnny Cash.

Now that I got a real good look at him, I realized that the reverend was dressed spiffier than usual. Instead of the usual black coat, he was wearing what looked to be a brand-new, black double-breasted jacket with a gray pinstripe. His sharply creased slacks looked to be of designer quality, and his shiny black Western boots sported tips that looked as if they might very well be genuine sterling silver. As if all this wasn't enough, he was also wearing a wide-brimmed black wool hat that cast a shadow over his face.

I couldn't help staring at that hat. The last thing you'd expect a man of the cloth to be wearing is a black hat. Hadn't anybody ever told the reverend that the men wearing the black hats in all the old movies were always the bad guys? Not to mention, hadn't anybody ever told him that folks generally didn't wear hats indoors? I put a big smile on my face anyway. "Why, Brother Tallman," I said, "I haven't seen you in—" I'd been about to say "a month of Sundays," but thank God I stopped myself just in time. Not wanting to bring up what could possibly be a sore subject, I finished, "—in a long time."

With a long, angular jaw, high, prominent cheekbones, and small, piercing blue eyes, Brother Tallman had the perfect face for a preacher. Not to mention the perfect nose. It was large and Roman with wide, flaring nostrils. No matter what you were doing, you could be sure that Brother Tallman's nose would not approve. You could be giving blood, making baked goods to send to Bangladesh, and boxing up all your clothes to donate to the Salvation Army—all at the same time, mind you—and Brother Tallman's nostrils would still be flaring. Even his own parishioners would admit that Brother Tallman was a tad hard to please. The way they put it, though,

the reverend was always looking at your im-
perfections and hoping for improvement. Less
tolerant folks around town put it differently.
They said that Brother Tallman was always
looking as if he were standing downwind from
a cow pie.

Brother Tallman was looking pretty much
like that now, to tell you the truth. I couldn't
decide if this was just his usual run-of-the-mill
disapproval, or if he was homing in on something specific. Like, oh, for example, what I'd
just said about Elmo, my own flesh and blood.

I grinned even wider. "Isn't it a beautiful
day? This sure is my kind of weather."

Like I said, it was cold, and murky, and
starting to drizzle, but I said this last with only
slightly less enthusiasm than someone announcing they'd just won the Kentucky lottery.
You've got to sound upbeat around Brother
Tallman. If you don't—if you look even the
slightest bit depressed or unhappy—it's a lot
like waving a sirloin in front of a pit bull.
Brother Tallman would suddenly be all over
you, giving you church pamphlets, quoting
Bible verses, and inviting—no, *demanding*—
that you attend his next church service. Everybody in Pigeon Fork knows that it doesn't take
much to set Brother Tallman off, too. A frown
is sometimes all it takes. Unless you're anxious
to spend a significant amount of time with
Brother Tallman, you'd better act real upbeat.

Why, I've seen an entire funeral home full of mourners turn downright cheerful the second Brother Tallman walked in the front door.

Brother Tallman didn't answer my enthusiastic greeting right away. Instead, he just kept standing there, staring at me. He did it for such a long time, saying absolutely nothing, that I began to feel downright uneasy. Maybe Brother Tallman really had heard every word I'd said about Elmo. Oh Lord. If he'd heard me, I was in for it.

Having Brother Tallman catch you sinning was even worse than having him catch you unhappy.

In fact, the last time I'd talked with Brother Tallman, I suddenly recalled, was sometime back in January, shortly after I'd discovered that the tire on the driver's side of my truck was flat. It had been at the end of a long day at work, I was totally exhausted, and yet I'd managed to deal with the entire situation in a mature, sensible way—I'd stood there for a minute or two, hollering obscenities at my truck.

Wouldn't you know, it had been during those few minutes of hollering that Brother Tallman had walked out of the bank across the street. The man must have had terrific hearing, or else I'd been hollering a lot louder than I thought. Either way, Brother Tallman had come striding over with the same frown on his face that he was wearing now. "You must ask for forgiveness, Brother Blevins," he'd said, pointing a bony finger in my direction. He'd been in the middle of the street by then, but his voice had carried, loud and clear, right to where I'd been standing.

"Get down on your knees right now," Brother Tallman had intoned, "and ask our dear Lord in heaven to forgive you for taking his name in vain."

I'd just looked at him. There had been, after all, quite a few people on the street all around us. I'd recognized Pop from Pop's Barbershop and Old Man Toomey, who owned the hardware store. Both men had been strolling down the sidewalk across the street. That is, they'd been strolling until they'd spotted Brother Tallman. After that, their strolling had picked up considerable pace. Both men had given me a quick look of sympathetic helplessness—the sort of look that you'd give somebody rapidly sinking in quicksand when you didn't have a rope on hand to throw him—and then both men had all but run in the opposite direction.

Pop and Toomey needn't have worried. Brother Tallman had been far too busy with me to notice them. He'd reached my side and placed a bony hand heavily on my shoulder. "Down on your knees, Brother Blevins," he'd said, his voice quavering up a storm. "Down, Brother, down!"

He'd sounded much like I sound myself

whenever I try to train my dog, Rip. I give this a shot from time to time. I try to get Rip to shake hands, or to fetch, or to do any one of a number of things that other folks seem to have taught their dogs. Each time, of course, my efforts end in total failure, once again proving the adage *You can't teach a young dog old tricks.*

"Get down on your knees, Brother. Now!" Brother Tallman had gone on.

I had been pretty sure I was wearing the exact same long-suffering expression on my face that Rip always gets on his during the training sessions.

"Reverend," I'd said, shaking my head, "I don't think so."

Brother Tallman's nostrils had flared. "But, Brother Blevins, you've got to cleanse your immortal soul!"

His hand had been getting heavier by the second. I'd shrugged it off. "Brother Tallman, I don't think my immortal soul is all that dirty."

Brother Tallman had taken that little pronouncement well. Raising his scrawny hands to the sky, he had all but yelled, "Repent, Brother Blevins, get down on your knees and repent!"

It had looked as if he wasn't about to give up. I'd taken a deep breath, and resigned myself. "Look, Reverend," I'd said. "Let me get my jack out of the back first. Then I can do my repenting while I'm down there anyway, changing the tire. That way, I'll be killing two birds with one stone, OK?"

Apparently, it wasn't OK. Brother Tallman's frown had deepened. Gazing heavenward, he'd said, his voice now loud enough to echo off hills in the distance and, oh, maybe, off the mountains of Tennessee, "Father, forgive this poor sinner, for he knoweth not what he do!"

I'd held up my hand. "You're wrong there, Reverend. I do, too, knoweth—"

I was actually smiling as I'd said this last, more or less trying to lighten up the whole situation, but evidently the reverend was not in a humorous mood. If, indeed, he ever got into one. Brother Tallman had glowered. "Brother Blevins," he said, his tone reproving, "your immortal soul is nothing to take lightly. Church services begin at ten on Sunday." Reaching into his pocket, he'd handed me a folded church bulletin with the words *Pentecostal Church of the Holy Scriptures* written at the top in Old English. That done, he'd cleared his throat, thrown back his head, and added, "Thou shalt not take the Lord's name in vain."

Oh, yeah, if Brother Tallman had heard what I'd been saying about Elmo when he came into the store, I was in for it for sure. He had stepped in front of the deodorant display, removed his hat, and was now leaning forward, twisting the hat in his hands, his scrawny neck stretching toward me. I braced myself.

"Brother Blevins." Oddly enough, the reverend actually lowered his voice. "I need to talk to you. Alone."

I stared at him. If he was trying to get me alone so that he could browbeat me into going to his church, I wasn't going to fall for it.

Not that I have any problem whatsoever with going to church, mind you. I'll admit I don't attend on Sunday the way I did when I was little, but back then my mom—God rest her soul—had been in charge of my churchgoing. Still, I'll have you know, I'd been a member of the Pigeon Fork Methodist Church for as long as I can remember. I hadn't even taken my name off the roll during the years I'd lived in Louisville. Mainly, I reckon, because it had made me feel as if a part of me had never left home.

No, it wasn't church I had a problem with—it was Brother Tallman's church, plain and simple. I had no doubt that Brother Tallman and all his parishioners firmly believed that they were right, which was fine by me. It was just that everybody who attended the Pentecostal Church of the Holy Scriptures seemed to think that they were super-duper right. So super-duper right, in fact, that all of them believed that if you didn't go to their church—the one and only Pentecostal Church of the Holy Scriptures right here in Pigeon Fork,

Kentucky—you were pretty much riding the express elevator marked Down, spiritually speaking. The Pentecostals were not about to cut you any slack for, oh, say, living in Australia, either. Nope, according to Brother Tallman and all the other Pentecostals, it was just your tough luck to have an ocean or two between you and the only right church on the planet. I reckon you could imagine, if Brother Tallman and his church were not any too tolerant of Australians, what they thought of Methodists and Baptists and Catholics. What they thought of those of the Jewish faith, or Buddhists, or Hindus, or anybody else, pretty much went without saying.

Actually, now that I think of it, it did not go without saying. Because if any of the Pentecostals got half a chance, they would definitely say it all right, out loud and everything. They would go on and on about how every single person in the world, except them, of course, was going straight to hell. The Pentecostals always said all this with a kind of malicious glee, too. For religious folk, the Pentecostals really seemed to get a kick out of condemning large segments of the population to eternal damnation. Amazingly enough.

I took a deep breath. "Brother Tallman, I'm real busy here." I indicated the carton of deodorant with a nod of my head.

Brother Tallman's nostrils quivered. "Brother

Blevins, I really need to talk to you." As he said this, he was looking around Elmo's Drugstore, his tiny eyes darting here and there, as if he were afraid somebody might overhear. He needn't have worried. It was a little after ten in the morning, and we were in the middle of the usual morning lull. Everybody who'd been intending to drop by to pick up a prescription or whatever on the way to work had already been in and gone. Right that minute there wasn't a soul in the place, except for Elmo and Melba Hawley—she's the secretary I share with Elmo—and they were both in the office at the back of the store. Elmo had himself a new computer program that was supposed to track profit and loss, and he was trying to teach Melba how to use it. The way I figured it, folks might never see Elmo or Melba again.

"I need to talk to you right now. *Professionally.*"

I stared at Brother Tallman. Professionally? Good Lord. Could it be that what the good reverend was talking about was business? *My* business, that is. An actual, honest-to-God— no pun intended—*job*?

Brother Tallman was now leaning even closer. "It's about a private matter," he whispered, still twisting his hat.

Well, well, well. I tried not to smile. In fact, I believe it was an indication of just what a gen-

uine professional I happened to be that I
somehow managed to resist my first impulse.
That impulse, of course, was to reply to
Brother Tallman in a voice loud enough to
carry all the way to the courthouse across the
street, WHAT? I'M NOT SURE I HEARD YOU
RIGHT. DID YOU SAY THAT YOU WANTED
TO TALK TO ME ABOUT A PRIVATE MAT-
TER, BROTHER TALLMAN? After the flat tire
incident, believe me, doing such a thing
would've felt good. Private investigation professional that I was, however, I only had to
swallow once before I was able to say in a
hushed whisper almost identical to Brother
Tallman's, "A private matter? Exactly what
kind of private matter?"

Hey, I know I sounded a tad suspicious.
You would think that, having not worked at
my chosen profession for half of an entire
year, I would be leaping at the chance that
somebody might've taken it into his head to
hire me. Matter of fact, I reckon I would've
been doing some major leaping had the
somebody been anybody but Brother Tallman. With Brother Tallman, there was a
50/50 chance that his "private matter" was
the current condition of my immortal soul.
His looking around the drugstore checking
for eavesdroppers was something he'd never
done before, but for all I knew, Brother Tallman had come up with a new gambit to get

me off by myself so he could really work me over.

Brother Tallman's nostrils were going to town. He looked definitely on the offended side as he said, "Brother Blevins, do I have to go into it with you right here? Where just anybody could overhear?"

I gave another quick glance around the store. It was still empty.

I turned back to Brother Tallman. "Yep," I said.

Brother Tallman's nostrils hated me. He took a long, deep breath, looked heavenward as if asking for strength, and then said, leaning so close to my ear that I could feel his breath on my face, "There's been an . . . uh . . . an irregularity in the church bank account."

I took a step away from the reverend and just looked at him. An irregularity? He made it sound like something you'd take Ex-Lax for. "What do you mean?"

Brother Tallman's eyes once again traveled all over the store before he answered. Finally, he said, "Well, Brother Blevins, uh, well—"

I decided to help him along. "Has somebody stolen from your church?"

I didn't say this particularly loud—I was still pretty much whispering—but Brother Tallman acted as if I'd just announced it over a PA system. The man actually went pale, and he staggered back a little. Glancing wildly around the store, he hissed, "For God's sake, SHUT UP!"

I just looked at him. Not being a preacher myself, I couldn't be sure, but hadn't the good reverend just taken the Lord's name in vain?

Brother Tallman stepped closer. "And you got it wrong. Somebody's been making deposits *into* the account."

I continued to stare at him. And then, without missing a beat, I came up with the kind of in-depth, incisive, cut-to-the-chase sort of question that, in my humble opinion, is the hallmark of my professional investigative career.

"Huh?"

2

For a religious sort, Brother Tallman didn't seem to be any too long on patience. In fact, it looked to me as if the entire story of Job had been pretty much lost on the good reverend. I'd no sooner said "Huh?" than Brother Tallman did a quick intake of breath.

"Brother Blevins," the reverend said, "I thought I made myself clear." His tone and nostrils were a tad testy. "I do *not* want to discuss this in public."

Me, I was looking around the drugstore again. In public? I sure couldn't see anybody in Elmo's except me, Brother Tallman, and the cardboard models on the women's makeup displays. So where exactly was all this public he was talking about?

"Could we go to your office?" Brother Tallman didn't wait for me to answer. He quickly added, his nostrils flaring to beat the band, "*Now?*"

I have no doubt that he thought that it was his getting testy with me that got me moving. The truth was, once Brother Tallman had let me know just how irregular his bank irregularity was, I was pretty anxious to hear all about it. "Sure, Brother Tallman, no problem," I said with a shrug. "Just let me put away this box, tell my secretary where I'm going to be, and I'll—"

The reverend did another quick intake of breath. "What? You're going to tell *Sister Hawley?*" His tiny blue eyes had gotten significantly bigger, and his nostrils looked like twin railroad tunnels now.

I knew, of course, why Brother Tallman had just said my secretary's name the way anybody else might've said the name Freddy Krueger. As I mentioned earlier, Melba Hawley is the secretary I share with my brother Elmo. This whole secretary-sharing thing was supposed to be a win-win situation for all of us. Melba would get a raise. Elmo wouldn't have to pay as much for Melba because I'd be paying part of her salary. And I would get my phone answered and my filing done without having to hire anybody full time. I even had it rigged so that my office telephone would ring down in the drugstore office, too. That way all Melba would have to do was punch a button to pick up the second line.

Like I said, it was supposed to be a good thing for all of us. There was just one hitch—Melba. She answers my phone just like she answers Elmo's. Hardly ever. What's more, she types and files just like she answers my phone. And, to be the secretary of a private eye, Melba is not all that private. Fact is, telling Melba anything is a lot like taking out an ad in the Pigeon Fork *Gazette*. Only the *Gazette* is slower at getting the word out.

At one time or another, I might as well admit, both Elmo and I have considered giving Melba her walking papers. The problem is, neither one of us has the nerve to do it. For one thing, she would not be above retaliation, and you know what they say about paybacks. For another, Melba provides the sole support of five children. Her husband Otis up and died of a heart attack a couple years ago. Of course, there are those who say that in Otis's case, that old joke is true. Otis isn't dead, he's hiding. Those that say this are generally those who've met the five small Hawleys that Melba refers to as her "young-uns." The rest of the town refers to them as her "hellions." Hellions or young-uns, Melba's offspring have added up to big-time job security for Melba. The way I figure it, Elmo and I can't possibly let Melba go until all her kids are out of high school, and from what I've heard regarding their academic progress, that might not be until a couple of them are in their thirties.

Given that I was pretty much stuck with Melba, I hoped that her loose lips were not common knowledge around town. If Brother Tallman knew, however, everybody in Pigeon Fork knew. I suppressed a sigh and quickly gave Brother Tallman what I hoped was a re-assuring smile. "All I intend to tell Melba is that I'm going to be upstairs in my office, OK? In case she needs to reach me."

Brother Tallman's nostrils continued to act up.

I ignored them and started to pick up the carton of deodorant at my feet.

Brother Tallman put a bony hand on my shoulder. "Brother Blevins," he said, "can't you just leave that carton where it is? I really do need to talk to you right this minute." His voice was so low that I had to lean toward him a little to make out what he was saying. "And do you really need to tell Melba where you're going to be? From what I hear, you don't get all that many calls anyways."

I tried not to wince at that one. Evidently, Melba's blabbermouth wasn't the only thing that was common knowledge around town.

The reverend's eyes were darting toward the front door again. "Brother Blevins, it really is urgent that I talk to you right away."

I hated to admit it, of course, but Brother

Tallman was right—my phone was not exactly ringing off the hook. So whether or not I told Melba where I was going to be probably didn't make a bit of difference. Not to mention the fact that this was Melba we were talking about. The woman who felt that just showing up pretty much met her end of the employment contract.

I made up my mind. "Let's go," I said.

Brother Tallman didn't waste any time. He turned and started to take off in the direction he'd come.

As it happened, that was the exact moment when the door to Elmo's office at the back of the store banged open and Melba herself came storming out. At five feet two and 250 pounds, believe me, she made quite a storm. She was all the way in the back of the store, and yet I could hear her just as clear as if she had been standing right next to me. "I'm a secretary, Elmo!" she was saying, "A seck-ree-tary! *That's* what I am!"

That, in my opinion, was subject to debate.

"I am *not* a computer programmer! You hear me?"

If Elmo hadn't heard Melba, he'd gone stone deaf in the last hour or so.

Melba wears her dark brown hair in a style that a lot of the women around Pigeon Fork apparently feel is a tried-and-true classic—the beehive. It looked to me as if, during the computer programming lesson, Melba's bees must've gotten a tad agitated. Her beehive was now setting a little sideways on her head, like maybe it had gotten knocked askew from the turmoil going on inside. Quite a few dark brown strands had come loose. Melba was tucking one particularly long strand behind one ear as she added, "—and I ain't interested in ever becoming no computer programmer neither!"

Elmo was only a couple of steps behind Melba. The computer lesson must've ended somewhat abruptly, because he still had a software box in one hand and what looked like a spiral-bound software manual in the other. "Now, Melba—," he said, his tone coaxing.

I think Elmo might've intended to say something more, but Melba cut him off. "Don't you 'Now, Melba' me," Melba said, turning briefly to waggle a sausage-like finger in Elmo's direction. "Learning that dumb program is not in my job description!"

Taking three-hour lunches wasn't in it either. Or letting the phone ring off the hook. Or hiding the filing she was supposed to do in the back of the file cabinet. And yet these glaring omissions from her job description had never bothered her before. Oddly enough.

"Now, Melba—," Elmo said again. At thirty-eight, Elmo is only four years older than me, but those four years must've been pretty rough. He's got red hair like mine, but he doesn't have much of it left. He's only got this orange-red border around his ears and the back of his head. On top, he has just nineteen hairs left. I know this for a fact. I counted them once when Elmo fell asleep on my couch watching a football game.

It's my considered opinion that Elmo's hair all fell out because he worries so much. All that energy constantly radiating from his brain must've totally fried his roots. He looked unbelievably worried now, running after Melba. His eyebrows were all jammed together, and his forehead looked like corrugated cardboard. "This here program's going to make things easy for you. It—"

"Easy, my foot!" Melba tossed over her shoulder. She was halfway down the aisle, rapidly heading in my direction.

Elmo, however, was gaining fast. "Melba, listen," Elmo said, "it says right here, 'New Version 4.3, with enhanced ease-of-use features . . .'" Elmo must've been desperate if he was trying to convince Melba by reading her the front of the software box, even as he hurried down the aisle after her. " '. . . automatically manages accounts payable, accounts receivable . . . and makes bookkeeping simple . . .'"

"*You're* simple if you think that I'm going to learn that stupid thing," Melba said over her shoulder. For a woman of her size, she can get around right smart. She deftly sidestepped the carton of deodorant now in her path and scooted right by me, obviously intending to put my body and the carton between her and my rapidly approaching brother. "Haskell, tell your simple brother that there is no way that I'm—," Melba said as she thundered by me. It must've been at this point that Melba caught sight of Brother Tallman. The reverend had only taken a step or two toward the front door when Melba and Elmo had come barreling out of the back office. Brother Tallman was now standing only a few feet away. Did I mention that his nostrils were flaring? He also added something new—his long, angular face went a dark red as he somberly watched Melba come to an abrupt halt.

Melba's mouth stopped as fast as her legs. Eyes widening, she made this sort of gulping sound, coughed once, and then, gathering her composure, she smiled so wide that you could see her back teeth. "Why, Brother Tallman, how nice to see you!" There was a lilt in Melba's voice now. "Beautiful day, isn't it?"

I shot a fast glance out the front windows. It was still gray and drizzling.

Turning to me, Melba added, smiling about as convincingly as a skull, "Isn't it a bee-you-tiful day, Haskell?"

"Gorgeous," I said.

Elmo caught up to us then. ". . . new user

friendly interface makes . . . ," Elmo was saying. Evidently, he hadn't seen Brother Tallman yet—probably because his eyes were focused on the software box in his hand. That was also, no doubt, why he ran smack-dab into the carton of deodorant I'd been emptying. The second he collided with it, Elmo let out a little yelp of pain and grabbed his right shin. "Damnation, Haskell!" Elmo said, hopping a little on his left foot and rubbing his leg with the edge of the software box. "Why the hell did you leave that damn box right in the middle of the aisle where anybody—"

Elmo must've spotted Brother Tallman right then, because much like Melba, he abruptly shut up. He also made an almost identical gulping sound. Then, clearing his throat, he said, "Why, Brother Tallman, good morning!" Elmo's mouth commenced smiling big time, but his eyebrows hadn't gotten the message. They remained all jammed together. "Beautiful day, isn't it?"

I glanced out the front window again. The drizzle had become a steady rain.

"Is there anything I can get for you, Brother Tallman?" Elmo went on. "Anything at all I can help you find?"

Brother Tallman looked straight at Elmo, then over at Melba. He seemed to be weighing in his mind whether or not he had time to point out their multiple transgressions. Apparently, he must've decided that saving Elmo's and Melba's immortal souls would have to wait. Brother Tallman sighed, looked real sad, and then finally said, "No, thank you, Brother Blevins. I'm just waiting on Brother Blevins."

Here, of course, Brother Tallman amply demonstrated the inherent problem in referring to everybody as Brother This or Sister That. If the Thises or the Thats happened to be big families—and a lot of farm families around these parts *were*—after a while you'd have no idea who in the world Brother Tallman was talking about. Fortunately, in this case, Brother Tallman made it clear exactly which Brother Blevins he was waiting on by casting a dark look in my direction.

All eyes, of course, followed the reverend's. With everybody staring at me expectantly, I took a deep breath. "Well," I said, reaching for the box at my feet, "I'll just put this carton away, and then—"

Elmo tapped me on the shoulder with a corner of his spiral-bound notebook. "Never you mind with that, Haskell. You go ahead," he said. He was still smiling from his eyebrows down, his tone magnanimous. "I'll put this carton away. You don't want to keep the reverend waiting, now do you?"

I stared at Elmo. His smile was starting to look pretty scary. "Well," I said, "if you really don't mind putting this away—"

"Don't mind at all!" Elmo said. "I'd be glad to do it! Glad!"

My goodness. What do you know. Maybe I ought to have Brother Tallman drop by more often. There was no telling what I could get Elmo to do just to hurry Brother Tallman out of his store.

I turned to Melba, who was at that moment looking holes through Brother Tallman. "Melba? I'll be in my office if anybody—"

Melba started nodding the moment I opened my mouth. "Yeah, yeah, yeah," she said, waving me off with one hand.

What professionalism.

Melba's small eyes were still resting speculatively on Brother Tallman. "So, Reverend," Melba said, "you got business here with Haskell?" Melba might've been trying to sound casual, but she was about as subtle as a wrecking ball.

Brother Tallman's lips tightened. He gave me a look that could possibly have broken a commandment or two, and then he said, "Sister Hawley, when somebody needs to talk to me, I consider it a sacred trust." As the reverend spoke, his voice took on the singsong tone that he always does when he's speaking from the pulpit. "I don't ask what it's about, I don't stop to wonder, I just answer. That's what I do, Sister. I just answer the call, much as our Lord would've done; I never stop to wonder, I never question, I know that I'm needed, and I want to—yes, Sister—I want to help. That's how every one of us should be, Sister, because we're all here to help each other, and when we're called, why, we . . ."

The reverend went on and on.

Melba was clearly sorry she'd asked. Elmo seemed pretty sorry, too. He was now glaring at Melba, and you could almost hear what he was thinking. *Now look what you've done!*

I, on the other hand, had been turning to head for the front door, but the reverend's impromptu sermon brought me up short. Wait a minute. Brother Tallman was making it sound as if *I* had called *him*.

I looked over at Melba. She was no longer staring holes through Brother Tallman; she was staring holes through *me*. I gave a little shrug, as if to say I didn't have any idea what the reverend was talking about, but that didn't seem to make any difference. Melba still stared at me, clearly trying to figure out what it was that I had to discuss with a minister.

I glanced over at Elmo. He was now staring straight at me, too, his eyes clearly questioning. I gave Elmo the same kind of shrug I'd just given Melba, and got pretty much the same results.

"That's right, Sister Hawley, I hear the call and I answer . . . ," Brother Tallman continued.

I decided I'd better interrupt before Brother Tallman passed around the collection plate. "Brother Tallman? I'll be heading on up to my office now."

I said it real casual-like, but the reverend got my drift right away. He stopped mid-sentence, nodded to Elmo and Melba, mumbled something real fast that sounded a lot like a benediction, and then turned to follow me.

We went out the front door at a pretty good clip. Out on the sidewalk, though, I pulled up short and turned around. "So what was that all about?"

Brother Tallman must've not been expecting me to brake, because he almost plowed right into me. He did manage to stop in time, but he looked a tad irritated as he answered me. "That was all about your not leaving when I asked you to, that's what. I think I made it very clear, Brother Blevins, that I wanted to talk in your office, but no, you had to wait until we had company."

OK, so I had transgressed. And yet it seemed to *me* that I wasn't the only one. "Brother Tallman, you told Elmo and Melba something that"—I stopped here, pretty much hesitant to call a man of the cloth an outright liar—"well, that was not exactly true."

Brother Tallman, believe it or not, actually looked surprised to have me say such a thing. "Oh no, Brother," he said, shaking his head, "you must've misunderstood me. For some of us, you see, telling a lie is impossible."

I just looked at him. If he started talking about George Washington and that cherry tree episode, this conversation was over.

"Let me explain, Brother," the reverend went on, putting his hand on my shoulder and smiling at me tolerantly. "I merely told Sister Hawley how I feel when one of my flock calls on me for help. That's all. Anything she thought after that was her doing. Not mine."

I just looked at him. It would appear that George Washington had the reverend here beat out bad in the truth department.

Brother Tallman was still smiling tolerantly as we climbed the stairs to my office. His smile faded, however, as he followed me into my office, sat down in the chair in front of my desk, and took a long, long look around.

To be honest—unlike the reverend, I might add—my office isn't as neat as it could be. Melba, as a matter of fact, calls my office the Bermuda Rectangle. According to Melba, it looks as if some mysterious force had sucked every paper scrap, every magazine, every candy wrapper, and every piece of junk mail from within a five-mile radius and scattered it all over every horizontal surface in the room.

Melba is exaggerating.

She is.

"So, Brother Tallman," I said, shoving the

stack of magazines on my chair onto the floor and sitting down, "you were telling me about a bank irregularity?"

It was Brother Tallman's cue to finish what he'd been telling me downstairs in the drugstore, but Brother Tallman didn't pick up on it. He was still looking around, his nostrils flaring so bad you might've thought there was a skunk hiding in here somewhere. When his eyes finally got back to me, the reverend was frowning. "Cleanliness, Brother Blevins, cleanliness is next to godliness," he intoned.

I just looked at him. "Yeah, I'd heard that," I said. "So. You were saying downstairs that somebody had made a deposit into your bank account? That sure doesn't sound like all that terrible a problem." It was, in fact, the kind of problem I could have all day long and never once complain about.

Brother Tallman just looked at me for a long moment. I couldn't tell if he was irritated at my having interrupted his sermon on the proximity of cleanliness to godliness, or if he was wondering if maybe I wasn't bright enough to grasp the complexity of his predicament. Either way, he looked as if he was fast running out of patience. *Again.* The man really did need to take another look at the Book of Job. "Brother Blevins," the reverend said, his tone downright testy again, "I can assure you, this *is* a terrible problem. Somebody has made a lot of deposits into the church account."

"A lot?" I repeated. "What do you mean, *a lot*? Exactly how many deposits are we talking here?"

Brother Tallman looked uncomfortable. He ran his hand through his thinning hair, took a deep breath, and finally said, "Thirty-two in all."

My head went up at that one. Brother Tallman was right. Thirty-two deposits was a *lot* of deposits.

"I can't believe the bank would let it happen *once*," the reverend was going on, "let alone thirty-two times." His mouth got pinched-looking again. "That they would let just *anybody* put money into the account—well, it's an outrage!"

I was pretty sure that bank security did not extend to preventing money from being deposited, but it didn't seem worth discussing. I rummaged around on my desk, finally found a small spiral-bound notebook under a stack of *Car and Driver* magazines, and started looking for something to write with. "How much money was deposited in all?"

Brother Tallman looked uncomfortable again. He shifted position in his chair before he said, "Brother Blevins, before I tell you how much, you've got to understand that this happened over a long, long, *long* period of time."

I nodded. I was patting down all the stacks

of paper and magazines on my desk, looking for lumps that could be a pencil or a pen. "So how much was it?" I asked again.

Brother Tallman shifted position again. "I mean, it started way back in December. That's when the first deposit was made. It showed up on my January statement."

I nodded again. I wasn't sure I'd call two months *a long, long, long time*, but that didn't seem worth discussing, either. "OK," I said, "I understand." I'd finished patting down the stuff on my desktop with no luck, and I started going through the drawers of my desk and checking inside. "So, how much money was—"

Brother Tallman interrupted me. "I also want to make it real clear that I was under the impression that these deposits were the work of the Lord."

That one got my attention. I stopped feeling around in my bottom right desk drawer, straightened up, and stared at the reverend. Had I heard him right? Did he actually think that God himself had been making deposits into his church account?

Brother Tallman was nodding. "I was sure that the Lord had reached out and touched one of His faithful."

I didn't say a word, but the way it looked to me, one of the faithful—as the reverend called him—might not be the only one who was touched.

"Our Heavenly Father just reached out, Brother Blevins," Brother Tallman hurried on, his voice doing that pulpit singsong again. "He just stretched out His big hand, and He touched one of His flock. Can you see it, Brother?"

Hey, I could see it. In fact, I believe Michelangelo had painted it on the ceiling of the Sistine Chapel.

"He just reached out and He asked for an offering of faith. That's what I was sure had happened. The Lord had asked for an offering, and one of His flock had answered. Whoever it was didn't need thanks, he didn't need praise, all he'd needed to do was answer the Lord. That's why whoever it was wanted to remain anonymous, because he was making an offering, Brother, he was—"

The way it was looking, if I didn't interrupt I wouldn't get the answer to my question until nightfall. "Brother Tallman, how much of an offering was it?"

If Brother Tallman's flaring nostrils were any indication, this was going to be good. "Well, it was"—the reverend cleared his throat and looked away—"it was two hundred thirty-five thousand, nine hundred and fifty-seven dollars."

"Good Lord!" I didn't mean to say this. It was just that I'd had no idea that what we were talking about was almost a *quarter of a million* dollars. I mean, that was some offering. If the reverend's theory was right, the Lord hadn't just touched somebody. He'd slapped him.

In the split second, however, after the "Good Lord" burst out of my mouth, I could see that Brother Tallman was gearing up. His nostrils were flaring big time, he was frowning even more, and he was taking a deep breath, in preparation, no doubt, to giving me his standard don't-take-the-Lord's-name-in-vain sermon.

I jumped in before Brother Tallman had a chance to say a word. "What I meant to say is that the Lord has certainly been good to you. That's what I meant by 'Good Lord.' Him giving you all that money and all. The Lord was truly good. He was wonderful, in fact."

OK. It wasn't a great save, but it was a save.

Brother Tallman stared at me for a good ten seconds, and then, apparently placated somewhat, he gave a little shrug. "Well, yes, Brother Blevins," the reverend said, "that's exactly what I thought. That the Lord had been real good, blessing me and my church this way. Up until this morning, that is."

"This morning?"

Brother Tallman nodded sadly. "I just called up the bank to get the current balance on the account, and—" He paused here and took a deep breath.

"And?"

"—and there's been a withdrawal."

I leaned back in my chair and just looked at the good reverend. Well, what do you know. The Lord giveth, and the Lord taketh away.

3

Brother Tallman's mouth looked pinched, as if every word he was saying was leaving a bad taste behind. "Somebody has withdrawn three thousand dollars. *Three thousand dollars!* That's why I've come to you. I need to find out what in heaven's name is going on."

It occurred to me that *what in heaven's name* sure did seem like the sort of phrase a minister would use, but I didn't say anything. I just sat there and nodded my head.

It also occurred to me that Brother Tallman had not come to see me before now. And, by his own admission, his bank "irregularity" had been going on for some time. I believed, then, that I could assume that as long as money was going *into* his bank account, Brother Tallman had no problem with it. It was only when money started going *out* that the good rev-

erend made up his mind to have this little odd-
ity looked into.

The reverend was now shaking his head sor-
rowfully. "It's an evil world we live in, Brother
Blevins, an evil, evil, evil world." Uh-oh. Four
evils in one sentence. And the reverend's voice
was taking on an appallingly familiar singsong
quality. "Anybody who would steal from a
church is capable of anything. *Anything*, Brother.
Oh, Lord, yes, you heard me, a person who
would steal from the House of God, why, he's the
worst kind of sinner! The *worst!*"

Wait a second now. I believe, off the top of my
head, I could come up with quite a few sinners
who could easily beat out a church-robber.
Hitler, for one, immediately sprang to mind.
Not to mention, hadn't the reverend just told me
that his church had been handed almost a quarter of a million dollars? Absolutely free? The
way I saw it, the Pentecostal Church of the Holy
Scriptures was still way ahead of the game.

"You know, Reverend, maybe the three thousand dollars wasn't really stolen," I said.
"Maybe whoever deposited the money just decided he needed some of it back—you know,
maybe he figured out that he'd given away a
little more than he meant to—so he made a
small withdrawal."

This seemed to me to be a perfectly logical
train of thought. If you could accept that
someone could actually give away a quarter of

a million dollars—which, for me, was a major leap of faith, no pun intended—then surely you'd also have to accept that this particular someone could take it back.

Brother Tallman, however, looked as if I was talking utter nonsense. "To begin with, Brother Blevins," he said, his tone reproving, "I would never call three thousand dollars a *small* withdrawal."

What could I say? He had a point.

"And," the reverend hurried on, "once a gift is given, it no longer belongs to the giver. He can't take it back because it's no longer his." The reverend's tone was now suggesting that he was stating the obvious. "Whoever took three thousand dollars out of my account is a thief. A *thief*, Brother. Just like the two sinners *crucified* with our Lord."

Judging from the relish with which he said the word *crucified*, I was pretty sure that Brother Tallman believed that this might be a fitting punishment for the current culprit.

His tiny eyes actually sparkled a little as he went on. "A low-down thief, just exactly like the men *nailed to the cross* on each side of our Saviour." The reverend now gave a little extra punch to the phrase *nailed to the cross*.

A change of subject clearly seemed to be in order. I cleared my throat. "So, tell me, Brother Tallman, what did Vergil have to say?"

Vergil Minrath is the sheriff here in Pigeon

Fork. I suppose I know him as well or better than anybody does around these parts. Back when my dad was still alive, Vergil and Dad were best friends. My mom died the year before my dad did, so I reckon Vergil is the closest thing I've got to a parent these days. Knowing Vergil as well as I do, I had no doubt that Vergil would agree with Brother Tallman on the crucifixion-of-thieves issue. Vergil might even want to get a hammer and do the nailing personally, being as how Vergil has always taken any infraction of the law within the boundaries of Crayton County as a personal affront.

"Did Vergil think that—"

I broke off when I caught the look on Brother Tallman's face. A muscle had started jumping in his angular jaw, and his nostrils were flaring up a storm all over again. "Brother Blevins," he said, "you don't seem to be paying attention." At this point, the reverend heaved an elaborate sigh. "Of *course*," he went on, his tone testy yet again, "I have not spoken to Sheriff Minrath about this. I believe I just told you that I want to keep things real quiet. I couldn't possibly have the sheriff nosing around, asking my parishioners all sorts of questions."

OK. I stood corrected. I took another deep breath. "Well, then, have you—"

Brother Tallman went right on as if I hadn't said anything. "Besides which, the sheriff could get the wrong idea. For all I know, he might actually start thinking that something could be going on, and then, well—"

Brother Tallman didn't finish, but he didn't have to. I knew what he was getting at. The reverend was afraid that Vergil might think that there was something crooked going on at the Pentecostal Church, particularly since it had recently come into an awful lot of money. I leaned back in my desk chair and stared at the reverend sitting opposite me, wondering just how valid that particular idea could be.

It's not that I really believed that a man of God could be pulling a fast one, but, hey, I had to consider the possibilities. After all, I'd been stung by clients before. In fact, judging from the number of times it had happened, you could get the idea that there were those in Pigeon Fork and vicinity who truly believed that I was stupid.

I certainly hoped the reverend here wasn't one of them.

The reverend was sitting up a little straighter now, meeting my gaze head-on. "It really is sad, Brother, how law enforcement folks are always so quick, so unbelievably fast, to jump to conclusions."

I wasn't sure if he was including me in the law enforcement folks group, or what. I deliberately tried to relax, slumping a little in my chair, so as not to look the least bit suspicious.

I must've looked more sleepy than relaxed, because the reverend frowned. "Are you paying attention to what I'm saying, Brother?"

I sat up a little straighter, nodding. "I'm hanging on every word."

Brother Tallman's nostrils didn't believe me. "What I'm *trying* to tell you," he said, frowning, "is that it is a crying shame, Brother, how law enforcement types always think the worst. Of course, you really can't blame them, what with the sin and degradation that they see every single day of their wretched lives—"

It was my turn to frown. I wasn't at all sure that I'd describe Vergil's life these days as *wretched,* and I most certainly wouldn't describe my life that way. Not since Claudzilla and I got a divorce, anyway. And particularly not since I met my girlfriend, Imogene Mayhew. Of course, the circumstances under which I met Imogene were, admittedly, of the wretched variety—I'd been investigating the murder of Imogene's sister, who'd been a client of mine—but once Imogene and I had gotten through that terrible time, our relationship had been amazingly free of wretchedness.

A thing which amazed me to this day.

Now that I thought about it, I wasn't any too clear on just how much sin and degradation Vergil and I got a gander at every day either. Unless, of course, you counted those soap operas on TV that I've caught Vergil watching more than once.

"I guess law enforcement types just can't help it," Brother Tallman was still going on, shaking his dark head sadly. "Peace officers are just that way."

Peace officers? Now there was a phrase I hadn't heard in a long time. Of course, I preferred it to those that I'd heard several times, back when I was a cop in Louisville: *Deputy Dog.* And *Freakin' Fuzz.* And, you know, other words that sound similar to *Freakin'.*

Brother Tallman was still shaking his head. "Yep, they always seem to think the very worst of their fellow man."

This from the man who reminded his congregation every week that everybody in the world was going to hell except them.

I took another deep breath. Yet another change of subject seemed to be in order. "So, have you talked to the bank about your problem?" I asked. "Did you ask Margaret or Earlene if they remembered who'd made the deposits?"

The Crayton County Federal Bank of Pigeon Fork only has two tellers, Margaret Mapother and Earlene Ford. There was not a doubt in my mind that if anybody had moseyed into Crayton County Federal, flashing a few thou that he wanted to deposit, Margaret or Earlene would've remembered it. And neither one of them would have any problem telling you all about it, either. In fact, word was around town that Margaret and Earlene had misinterpreted their job titles. They both apparently felt that what tellers did was tell—pretty much anything and everything they knew.

At the mention of Margaret and Earlene, Brother Tallman looked appalled. The muscle in his long, angular jaw started jumping big time. "Brother Blevins, you're not getting it. I want to do nothing that would draw attention to this problem. *Nothing*. Do you understand? I can't have my parishioners wondering if there's something strange going on with the church money. Now, do you understand?"

I was nodding even before Brother Tallman finished speaking. "I understand perfectly," I said. I did, too. I understood real clear that if the members of his church started worrying about the church money, Brother Tallman stood a real good chance of passing around the collection plate and having it come back empty.

The reverend was now leaning forward, and his small piercing eyes looked even more piercing than usual. "I've asked around town, Brother, and I know what you charge. Thirty dollars an hour, or two hundred dollars a day. I'm ready to give you two days' pay up front in cash, but first, I need to know something."

I just looked at him. I know I should've been tickled pink at even the possibility of two full days' pay in advance. To tell the truth, I know I would have been, had I not already heard how much money Brother Tallman currently had at his disposal. Ever since the reverend had told me that, I'd been pretty much planning on upping the ante, so to speak, when he asked me how much I charge. Not that I'd intended to do anything underhanded, mind you. Thirty dollars an hour or two hundred dollars a day is downright cheap for detective work even in this part of the country. There's been many a time, in fact, that I've been tempted to add the words *Discount Detective* to the sign on my front door. No, charging Brother Tallman a fee more in line with what detectives make in Louisville would only have been fair.

Only now, of course, I realized I couldn't get away with it.

The reverend was still staring holes through me. "What I need to know, Brother Blevins, is this: Are you a *private* private detective or not?"

I might not have been able to give myself a little raise, but four hundred dollars, no matter how you sliced it, was a tidy sum. I drew myself up, and yes, I admit it, I was a tad embarrassed to hear myself say what I was about to say. But I did it anyway. "Oh, I'm a *private* private detective, all right. Yes, indeed, I most certainly am a very private private detective."

I also happened to be an idiotic idiot.

Brother Tallman acknowledged what I'd said with a brief nod of his head. "OK, then," he said. He pulled at the cuffs of his double-breasted coat, flicked what looked to me like nonexistent lint off his sleeve, and then took a deep breath. "It wouldn't do me any good, Brother," he said, "to talk to Margaret and Earlene, because according to my bank statement, none of the deposits were made here in Pigeon Fork. The deposits were all made at the branch in E-town."

E-town is what a lot of Kentucky residents call Elizabethtown. Located between here and Louisville, E-town is about twenty miles north of Pigeon Fork, if you're traveling on Interstate 65. Even though it's more than ten times the size of Pigeon Fork, E-town still qualifies as a small town. I reckon that makes Pigeon Fork minuscule.

"*All* of the deposits were made in E-town?" I asked.

Brother Tallman nodded. "Every single one of them. I brought along my bank statements, so's you can see for yourself."

With that, he reached into an inside pocket of his black suit coat, produced a couple of fat envelopes, and handed them over. I glanced through their contents. Each envelope contained a bank statement dated the sixth of the month, one for January and one for February. There were cancelled checks included in both envelopes, but no deposit slips. Apparently, the bank did not return the slips, it just itemized the deposits on the statement. Not having the original deposit slips, there was no way to get a look at the handwriting on the things, no way to get any real clue as to who might've made any particular deposit. No way, even, to ascertain that the deposits had all been made by the same person.

The January envelope contained nineteen cancelled checks. The February envelope contained forty-one. I gave each statement a quick going-over. Just as Brother Tallman had said, the deposits had begun in December. On December 9, to be exact, a deposit of $3,000 had been made at the Crayton County Federal branch in Elizabethtown. The notation beside the figure indicated that the deposit had been in cash. After that, the deposits were made in varying amounts, never less than a thousand dollars, and sometimes several times more. There didn't seem to be any pattern to the deposits, as best as I could tell. There'd be deposits day after day after day, and then for the next two or three days there'd be none. Sometimes, more than one deposit had been made in one day. The last deposit on the statement had been made on February 5. It was now February 11.

I looked up at Brother Tallman. "This February statement ended on the sixth. You might've had some more deposits since then."

Brother Tallman's nostrils flared once again. "Well, of *course*, I might've had some more deposits since then. Just look at the statements. There have been deposits made into this account nearly every single day."

Crayton County Federal doesn't have a drive-in window, or an anytime teller machine. According to Harve Parnell, the bank president, the thinking here is that the bank never wants to lose the personal touch. It always wants to maintain a hands-on relationship with its customers. In my opinion, however, the thinking here is more likely to be *We're not going to baby you.* If you want your damn money, get out of your damn car and come in and get it, you lazy son of a gun.

This personal touch philosophy makes it pretty difficult to check your current balance anonymously. Still, I had to ask. "Brother Tallman, have you called the bank to see if any more—"

I should've known by then what the reverend's answer was going to be. "Brother Blevins," he said, his nostrils flaring again, "do you have a hearing problem? It's like I just said, I don't want folks talking about the church money, understand? And, as sure as I'm sitting here, if I call the bank asking questions, why, it'll be all over town in a heartbeat."

I would've liked to have objected to that one, but the truth was, the reverend was right. In spite of everything the Crayton County Bank folks told you about how they guarded their customers' privacy, the reality was that the bank was smack-dab in the middle of a minuscule small town. And minuscule small towns are notorious for the way everybody seems to know everybody else's business.

Margaret and Earlene would not actually *intend* to tell everybody in Pigeon Fork all about the financial goings-on at the Pentecostal Church of the Holy Scriptures, but they'd manage to do it anyway. What would happen was that each of them would probably tell just one other person, swearing them to secrecy. And those two people would tell two other people, swearing *them* to secrecy. And those two would tell another two, and, well, you get the picture. Before long, every man, woman, and child in Pigeon Fork would be keeping the exact same secret. Which would hardly be a secret anymore.

I began leafing through the two sets of cancelled checks. Let me see, nineteen checks in the January statement, mostly written in December, forty-one checks in the February statement, mostly written in January . . . I glanced up at the minister. Oddly enough, this time he did not meet my gaze head-on but bent instead to flick what looked to me to be nonexistent lint off his black slacks. "Uh, Brother Tallman," I said, trying to sound real casual, "you seem to have written quite a few more checks in January than you did in December. And you'd kind of expect it to be the other way around, considering Christmas and all."

No surprise, Brother Tallman's nostrils flared once again. "Well, of *course* I've written some checks." His tone implied that if I didn't know that, I was not the detective I pretended to be. "There *are* church expenses, you know. Heat, water, and things like that. And then there's Sister Tallman's and my living expenses."

"Uh-huh." That's all I said. I was looking through the cancelled checks while Brother Tallman was talking. One was to Ye Old Tyme Religion Bookstore.

The reverend was now brushing nonexistent lint off his slacks again. "We had to replace some hymnals this month . . . the old ones had gotten awful ragged . . ."

I glanced back down at the bank checks. Right after the check to the bookstore, there was one for $1,255 made out to Rodes. The only Rodes I knew was a men's clothing store in Louisville, Kentucky. Back when I was living in Louisville, I'd actually been in Rodes a couple of times. I'd never actually bought anything there, of course, mainly because I never could quite convince myself that one measly tie could ever be worth $75. Not to mention, I wasn't rightly sure that I'd ever be comfortable wearing a suit that cost more than the down payment on my house. I took another look at the reverend's black suit. And his black hat. They sure did look nice. Real nice. Like, oh, say, $1,255 worth of niceness.

The reverend was still going on. ". . . and then there were, you know, assorted incidentals . . . this and that . . ."

I'd gotten to the last of the checks, and I started doing a little fast arithmetic in my head. Unless I'd added wrong, Brother Tallman's this-and-thats and assorted incidentals totalled almost four thousand dollars.

"It's not like Sister Tallman and I are wealthy, you know," Brother Tallman added. "We barely get by. We're not like Jim Bakker used to be, or Jerry Falwell . . ."

He pronounced the name as if it were spelled *Foul*well.

"Uh-huh." That's all I said. I didn't say it any special way, either. I really didn't. I was wondering, of course, what exactly Jesus would have thought of one of his spokesmen who, having suddenly come into a chunk of change, immediately ran out and got himself some new duds, instead of, oh, say, donating the money to a soup kitchen, or buying a few odds and ends for the poor.

On the other hand, you could look at the situation like this: Before the reverend got all this money, he himself was one of the poor. So spending the money on himself was exactly the same as donating it to the poor.

Yeah. Right.

I put all the checks and each statement back into their appropriate envelopes, and handed them back to the good reverend.

Brother Tallman must've picked up on what was going through my mind, because as he tucked the envelopes into an inside coat pocket, he started to sound downright defensive.

"Look, before I got this money, I hadn't had me a new suit in I don't know how long. And I knew, Brother, I knew that God had sent me this money for a purpose. A *purpose*, Brother. Yes, Lord YES, I knew that I had been sent this blessing because He wanted His servant to look good."

I blinked at that one.

"That's right, Brother Blevins, because I'm like an advertisement for the Lord—that's what I am—a walking, talking, living, breathing advertisement for the Lord, and what kind of message am I sending if I'm walking around in a worn-out coat?"

I was tempted to remind him that, from everything I'd heard about Him, Jesus Himself had not exactly been a snappy dresser, but I had no doubt that broaching that little subject would only prolong this little discussion. Once again it appeared to be time for a change of subject.

I cleared my throat again.

"So, who has access to the church check-book?"

Brother Tallman frowned. "Why do you need to know that?"

That one set me back a little. Mainly because the reason seemed pretty obvious to me. "I need to know who might have been able to take some of your bank deposit slips without anybody noticing."

Brother Tallman's frown deepened. "Haskell—," he began.

Of course, the second he called me by name, I knew I was in for it. It was the first time he hadn't called me Brother Blevins.

"—the Pentecostal Church of the Holy Scriptures is a house of worship."

I just looked at him. Well, that would certainly explain the name.

"It's a temple," the reverend went on. He was building steam, his voice beginning to rise and fall like the tides.

"And there is nobody—*nobody*, mind you—who attends my church who could've done this. None of my flock would even be capable of doing such a thing. Why, accusing one of them would be, well, it would be blasphemy!"

I blinked at him again. Over the course of my life I have been accused of many things, but blasphemy had never been one of them.

I cleared my throat and tried for a casual

tone. "Uh, Reverend, you do know that in order to investigate this case, I'm going to have to go talk to the bank, and after that, I'll need to talk with anybody who had access to your bank statements."

Amazingly enough, Brother Tallman looked shocked. "Whatever for?"

I blinked again. "Reverend, that's pretty much how a case like this is investigated. You—"

Brother Tallman cut me off, his small eyes shooting sparks. "Look, if *that's* all you're going to do—if you're just going to bother folks with a lot of questions—well, *I* could've done that. What the hell do I need to hire you for, if I could do it myself? I thought you were a professional, I thought—"

I wasn't sure, but it seemed to me as if the reverend here was sounding more and more unchristian. I think Brother Tallman must've suddenly noticed how he sounded, too, because he stopped right in the middle of what he was saying and took a deep breath. "OK," he said. "OK. What I meant to say," he went on, his tone even again, "is that I was under the impression that you private investigation professionals would know how to look into this in a real discreet kind of way."

I just looked at him. The man wanted me to find out who had taken his money, but he wanted me to do it without talking to anybody at his bank or at his church? Oh, yeah, *that* ought to be easy. Was there anything else he wanted? Like, oh, say, did he want me to walk on water?

On the other hand, the reverend was going to give me two full days' pay. For starters.

I sat up even straighter. "Oh, I understand now," I said. "What you want is an *undercover* operation."

The reverend blinked his tiny eyes. "Undercover?"

I nodded. "So that nobody catches on to what I'm doing." I nodded even more vigorously. "Oh yeah, undercover is the way you want to go on this one."

Brother Tallman was already nodding. "Undercover," he repeated to himself. As if it were a word he'd never heard before, but he really liked the sound of it.

I was both nodding and smiling now. "Yep, I've done quite a few of these here undercover jobs, and they're the only way to go when you want your investigation to be kept under wraps."

Brother Tallman's nodding accelerated. "Yes, Brother, yes, indeed, you should investigate this undercover!"

I continued my nodding, trying to keep time with the reverend's. "I'll just act as if I've come by to consult you on church business, and then when nobody is looking, I'll have me a look-see at your office setup."

Brother Tallman looked eager now. "Great! Why, we can head out there right now—"

I smiled. I started to get to my feet, and then I thought better of it. "Oh," I said, "there *is* one other thing."

Brother Tallman's nostrils flared anew. "One other thing?" he asked.

I leaned forward. And, yes, I admit it, I was feeling a tad bothered by the reverend's spending what looked to me to be clearly church funds on designer duds.

My smile grew even wider. "Undercover is extra," I said.

Brother Tallman's face fell.

4
§

Before Brother Tallman and I left to pay his church a little visit, he surprised me twice. The first surprise was when he paid me up front.

This is something I always try to get clients to do, but they hardly ever actually do it. Let me tell you, it's always a good idea to have the money in your hands *before* you get all involved in a case and dig up some information your client might not want to hear. If you don't already have your fee in your pocket and you end up telling your client some things he isn't any too grateful to hear, he might not pay you at all. This, I reckon, is a variation on that old "kill the messenger" scenario. Only in this case, instead of killing the messenger, unhappy clients pretty much go after my wallet.

To prevent this from happening, I always

make an effort to get as much of my money up front as possible. When Brother Tallman asked me how much extra an undercover operation would be, I didn't hesitate. "It's twice as much," I told him with one of my best disarming smiles.

At least, I thought it was one of my best. I might've been wrong, though, because Brother Tallman did not return my smile. "Double?" he said. "Undercover is *double*?"

Once again I didn't hesitate. "That's pretty much standard for the entire detecting industry," I said. Actually, I didn't have the slightest idea whether this was standard or not. I wasn't even sure detective work *was* an industry, but I didn't waver when the reverend's nostrils started acting up again.

"You are telling me that doing undercover work costs two times as much as regular detective work?" I could've been oversensitive, but the reverend seemed to be questioning my integrity.

If I hadn't been lying, the reverend's attitude might have hurt my feelings. As it was, however, I just shrugged. "Yep," I said, "that's what I'm telling you, all right. Everybody in this business charges twice as much for undercover." I tried to convey by my tone that I agreed with him, that it was indeed a rip-off, and that even though I sincerely longed to change the industry standard, I was powerless to do so. Rules were rules, you see. "It's a damn shame," I added, shaking my head sympathetically.

The reverend did not look the least bit moved by my sincerity. At this point, however, he surprised me for the second time. Frowning, he reached unceremoniously into an inside pocket of his black designer jacket and withdrew a wad of bills. I couldn't help but stare. On top of the stack was a hundred-dollar bill.

My mouth actually went dry. Good Lord. The last time I'd seen that much money in somebody's hand, I'd been playing Monopoly as a kid.

"You're paying me in *cash?*" I said.

Brother Tallman gave me a contemptuous look. "Of course I'm paying you in cash," he said. "I can't very well write you a check, can I?"

I reckon I'm a little slow. I just looked at him blankly, wondering if he had some kind of writing problem, like, oh, say, carpal tunnel syndrome, until Brother Tallman rolled his eyes. "Brother Blevins," he said, his tone getting downright testy again, "I can't believe I'm having to tell you this again."

I was real quick with the comeback this time. "Tell me what?"

Brother Tallman rolled his beady little eyes again. "Look, I don't want anybody knowing that I've hired you. Understand? I don't want there to be any record of it. None. So, no, I won't be writing you a check." Once again his tone indicated that he was stating the obvious.

He peeled off some bills, handed them to me, and got to his feet. "Now can we get on with this?"

I tried not to gawk at the money in my hand. *Eight* hundred-dollar bills.

We got on with it.

I keep my Ford pickup parked in the alley between Elmo's and the Pigeon Fork Dry Goods Store next door, so in a matter of minutes, I was in my truck, following Brother Tallman out of town.

The Pentecostal Church of the Holy Scriptures is only about five miles out of town, if you turn left on Highway 46 off of Main Street. If you keep on going down Highway 46, eventually you'll end up at the church's campground, where they hold their revival meetings and their retreats and Lord knows what all. No pun intended, of course.

I've always been under the impression that it was only after you passed the Pentecostal Church of the Holy Scriptures Campground that you knew beyond a shadow of a doubt that you'd finally arrived in God's country. Beyond the campground there is nothing but trees, trees, and more trees. And rolling countryside. Dotted, of course, with assorted cows and pigs and the like.

The Pentecostal campground is well known

around these parts, it being the place where one of Brother Tallman's church members had himself a vision following a particularly inspirational revival meeting. According to the story, which spread like wildfire through the town, this particular church member—who, incidentally, has never been named—actually witnessed the twelve Apostles setting up camp right there among the tall trees of the one and only Pentecostal Church of the Holy Scriptures Campground.

This, of course, has made the campground pretty much the equivalent of Lourdes for the members of Brother Tallman's church. For nonmembers, the campground has become more like the best joke they've ever heard. A joke so funny, in fact, that all you have to do is repeat just two words of it, and folks will burst out laughing. Those two words are, of course, "camping disciples." Yessirree, that one's a real knee-slapper. At least, it's a knee-slapper with everybody in town except the members of Brother Tallman's flock.

I let a truck and a car get between me and Brother Tallman as I followed his van down Highway 46. It wasn't as if I didn't already know where we were going, and even if I didn't know, I couldn't have lost sight of his vehicle even if I'd wanted to. Brother Tallman drives a large, white Ford van with the name of his church painted in large blue letters on both sides. In addition to the church's name, which is not exactly short, there's also the church's address, the church's phone number, and the words Sunday Worship 10 AM on both sides. This, of course, makes for an awful lot of reading as this thing is whizzing by you on the highway. Fact is, I reckon the church van would be a real traffic hazard if folks really did try to read everything that's written on the thing. Folks around Crayton County, though, already know what the van has got to say, so they pretty much don't even give it so much as a passing glance.

Thank heaven. No pun intended once again.

You might think that, what with there being so many words on each side of the van, those words would necessarily have to be in awful small type. In order to fit them all in. That isn't true, though. Mainly because the Pentecostal Church van is pretty big. At one time the word around town was that the entire Pentecostal Church could be transported in this particular vehicle at any one time. That, however, was before the camping disciples story got started. After that little press release, the church membership grew quite a bit. These days it would probably take three or four vans to cart them all around.

You can tell the church membership has grown, too, because there are quite a few Pentecostal Church bumper stickers around town.

That, I might as well admit, was why I let a couple vehicles get between me and Brother Tallman's van. I was getting pretty tired of looking at his bumper sticker.

Of course, I'd been pretty tired of looking at these stickers long before today. In white lettering on a purple background with a cross on each side of the lettering, the bumper sticker reads I BRAKE FOR SINNERS.

Brother Tallman just loves that bumper sticker, enough so that he's handed them out to all his church members and just about anybody who will take one. I've actually seen a few stuck on the front of high schoolers' notebooks, and one plastered to the forehead of a kindergartner.

Brother Tallman will be more than happy to tell you that the idea for this bumper sticker was heavenly inspired. "It just came to me. Just like the day I was called into the ministry. I just knew. Just like that, all of a sudden I knew exactly what the Heavenly Father wanted that bumper sticker to say."

It was still hard for me to swallow the fact that God would take time out from doing everything else He had to do—like, oh, say, trying to stave off famine in Third World countries—to pen a bumper sticker. What's more, even if I accepted that God would actually stoop to bumper-sticker creation, I still had a problem with this particular sticker. The implication of this thing seemed to be that

Brother Tallman, of all people on earth, had been entrusted with the responsibility of recognizing who amongst us was doing the sinning. I believe the inherent danger of the reverend's braking suddenly every time he spotted a transgressor pretty much goes without saying.

I reckon it's the smugness of this sticker that bothers me most. The idea that any human being down here thinks that he is capable of doing a thumbs-up, thumbs-down on the rest of humanity seems a tad presumptuous to me.

It took a lot longer than you might think to get to the Pentecostal Church because the speed limit on the narrow two-lane blacktop Brother Tallman and I were traveling is only forty miles per hour. It's real easy to figure out why the speed limit is so low, though. Anybody who'd go any faster than forty on all the hairpin curves and roller-coaster dips is just plain suicidal.

For all the dips and curves, there are quite a few businesses located on Highway 46, particularly within the first five miles or so outside of town. We passed Guenther's Used Cars, the Crayton County District #2 Firehouse, the First Baptist Church, and Culvert's Wrecker Service, among others.

We didn't pass all that many houses. With regard to houses, however, I reckon Highway 46 is no different from any other country road around these parts. On this road you'll find huge homes with parklike lawns, an in-ground pool out back, and a satellite dish out front. These opulent homes, however, will be right across the street from a tiny frame farmhouse badly in need of paint, with an ancient washing machine sitting out on its sagging front porch.

I think this is one of the reasons I like these winding country roads. They keep folks from getting uppity.

Up ahead Brother Tallman made a sharp left-hand turn into a wide gravel parking lot, and I followed right behind him. There were two other vehicles in the lot already—a red late model Toyota Tercel and a light green Aspire. I recognized the Aspire as Sister Tallman's car. Of course, even if I hadn't already known it was her car, I might've guessed. The Aspire had the church's phone number painted in bright red on both doors. The phone number was right under the words Get in Touch with God. I may be leaping to conclusions here, but it seemed to me as if this sentence appearing right next to the number could possibly give folks the idea that God was answering the phone at the Pentecostal Church of the Holy Scriptures. Of course, this could have been exactly the impression that the good reverend wanted to give.

As I pulled up next to the reverend's van and parked, I took a long look at the Pentecostal

Church and thought what I always do every time I see the thing.

It sure doesn't look like any kind of church I'd recognize.

What it looked like was a redbrick elementary school. An elementary school all on one floor that just happened to have a huge white cross stuck on the front—right next to the double front doors—and several long stained glass windows facing the road. Of course, the fact that the building had actually been an elementary school before the Pentecostal Church had taken up residence there could possibly be the reason I kept seeing it as a school rather than a church. Crayton County had consolidated some school districts and closed some schools, and this here building had housed one of the elementary schools that had gotten the axe. From what I'd heard, the Pentecostal Church had bought the building for a song. Or as some folks around town put it, for a hymn.

In fact, up until a year or so ago, the only thing at all churchlike around the Pentecostal Church was that big cross out front. And it seemed so out of place on the front of the long, low brick building that it looked as if maybe it was just one of the white crosses folks put by the side of the road to indicate that a fatal car crash occurred at that spot. Only, in this case, the white cross on the front of the building was so big that it made you think that maybe there had been a multi-car pileup in the very parking lot I'd just pulled into.

Last year Brother Tallman and his flock must've finally noticed that their church was sorely lacking in church ambiance. They had recently done some major fund-raising, so they bought a bunch of stained glass windows to replace what had been ordinary glass panes on the front of the building.

I couldn't say the stained glass exactly did the trick. It just looked as if maybe the kids who had attended this elementary school had colored with Magic Markers on the windows.

Reverend Tallman had already gotten out of his van and was waiting for me on the sidewalk. Leading the way through the double doors, he said, "Brother Blevins, the office is right this way."

He really didn't have to show me. The church office was now where the old school office had been, and you couldn't exactly miss it. It was the first door we came to, and the only door with a small sign that still said VISITORS MUST SIGN IN.

I wondered if I should ask for a hall pass.

As Brother Tallman headed into the office, with me right in back of him, he was saying, "All the financial stuff—you know, the checkbook and stuff like that—it's kept right in here in my desk—" At this point he stepped inside, and instantly his tone changed. "—And I'm so glad, Brother Blevins, so truly glad that you came to me in your hour of need. Because this is what I'm here for, Brother. *Ask and ye shall receive*, that's what the Good Book says, so if you ask, you better get ready to receive. Lord, yes, *that's* what I'm here for, Brother—"

I couldn't help but stare at him. Brother Tallman had slipped into singsong mode, his voice rising and falling as if pulled hither and yon by some powerful emotional tide. "Brother Tallman?" I'd been about to ask him what in the world he was talking about, but as soon as I followed the reverend through the door, I had my answer. He wasn't talking about anything. He was giving me a cover.

Because just inside the door we had ourselves some witnesses.

There were, in fact, two women standing behind the counter in the church office. They had apparently been deep in conversation, but they broke off to stare at the reverend and me.

"Brother Blevins," Brother Tallman said. "You remember Sister Tallman, don't you?"

I nodded. The reverend's wife would've been hard to forget, but I had no doubt that there were those who'd tried. In her late forties, she would've been described as average—average height, average build—except for one thing. She had the thinnest lips I believe I'd ever seen. Sister Tallman also seemed to pride herself on never wearing any makeup whatsoever, so you couldn't help but notice just exactly how thin her lips were. Being as kind as possible, I'd have to say that her lips were so thin her nose looked as if it had been underlined.

Sister Tallman was wearing the sort of dress she always seemed to wear—thick and long and high. Made of thick blue corduroy, the dress's skirt was long enough to reach her ankles, and its ruffle collar was high enough to touch her chin. Its sleeves had corduroy ruffles that extended almost to her knuckles. Let's face it, doctors have gone into surgery less covered up than Sister Tallman. The only thing even close to attractive about the woman was her hair—it hung to her waist in thick chestnut waves.

"Good afternoon, Sister Tallman," I said.

Her response was a quick nod, an even quicker tightening of her already thin lips, and a curt "Good afternoon." Her eyes darted to her husband, and something in that glance told me that she knew exactly why I was paying the church a little visit. She did not look all that delighted with the idea.

"And this is our church secretary, Sister Ivalene Dank," Brother Tallman was going on.

I nodded at Sister Dank much as I had at Sister Tallman. You'd think Ivalene would be a real uncommon name, but believe it or not, this was not the first time I'd ever met somebody called Ivalene. Back in high school, I'd known an Ivalene Fish. The poor girl had endured four long years of being called Valvoline and Halvoline, and sometimes—for reasons I have yet to figure out—Penzoil. I have no doubt that she would've shortened her name to just Iva except that she must've realized that it would do no good whatsoever to change her name to Iva Fish. There was also the distinct possibility that things might've gotten worse.

"Glad to meet you, Sister," I said.

Sister Dank didn't answer me right away. She was looking over at Brother Tallman, then over at me, and then back to Brother Tallman, her eyes frankly curious. The woman looked to be about my age—in her mid-thirties. She was about the same height and weight as Sister Tallman, but the most accurate word to describe Sister Dank's face was rounded. She didn't seem to have a single sharp feature. In fact, it looked as if maybe her face had melted, and in the process, every edge had been rounded off. Her hair was much like that of Sister Tallman only it was bigger. It stood out from her face in a mass of brown curls, and hung almost to her waist.

She had a perpetual sleepy look, too. She looked at me from beneath half-closed lids, and said, "Gladtameetyatoo," making it sound like all one word. Her tone was bored.

Sister Dank was wearing an outfit that a lot of women in Pigeon Fork seem to think is appropriate for all occasions: the sweat suit. Apparently these women feel that since it's got the word *suit* in the name, sweat suits are appropriate for office wear and pretty much any other business occasion. I did have to admit, however, that Sister Dank's suit was better than a lot I'd seen. At least it didn't have any holes in embarrassing places. Or the Budweiser logo on the back with the words This Butt's for You stenciled across the rear. This last style has been amazingly popular around town, and considering the size of some of the stencil areas, pretty scary. I believe it was a testament to Sister Dank's fundamental sense of class that she had managed to resist following the current fashion trend. Her sweat suit was a sedate navy blue.

"So you're here to see Brother Tallman, are you?" she went on, her sleepy eyes widening just a little as she looked back at me.

Brother Tallman didn't give me time to answer. "That's right. Brother Blevins and I will be in my office." He indicated with a nod of his head a door down the hall in back of the women. "Come on, Brother, I reckon with what you want to discuss, you'll want a little privacy."

I just looked at him. What on earth was he talking about?

The reverend must've noticed how my eyes bugged out a little as I stared at him, because he hurried on. "Oh my yes, it really ain't something that should be talked about in front of the ladies, you know—"

I blinked a couple times at that one. Oh. Now, I got it. Well, thank you so much, Reverend, for throwing me under the bus. He was making it sound as if *I* were the one who'd called him. To confess something that apparently had been weighing on my conscience. Something that, from the sound of it, sounded pretty deviant.

"—so, Brother Blevins," the reverend went on, "if you'll follow me . . . we'll close the door, and then while you and I talk, these nice ladies won't be able to hear a word—"

Oh for God's sake. Evidently, whatever it was that I was supposed to have done was enough to sully the ears of nice women. I believe it goes to show what a consummate professional I am that I didn't interrupt him to say, *Oh no, Reverend, I'd love to discuss it out here. No problem with that at all.*

I gave Sister Dank a quick glance. Her eyes, which appeared to be riveted to my face at this point, no longer looked sleepy in the least.

Even Sister Tallman was staring at me now as if maybe she was reconsidering whether or not she'd been wrong about the reason she'd thought at first that I was here. That maybe, instead of looking into the church's bank irregularities, I'd just dropped by to discuss the unnatural relationship I'd been having with my dog Rip.

There didn't seem to be any way to get out of this one. I was, after all, supposed to be undercover, for which the good reverend had paid double. I tell you, though, if I'd had any idea just how deep undercover I was going to be, I'd have charged a *lot* more.

The reverend was moving past the counter, and, feeling like a misbehaving kid on his way into the principal's office to be paddled, I started to follow him. Unfortunately, the second I moved, Sister Tallman suddenly clasped her hands together. "Oh you sweetheart!" she crooned. "Come here to mama, you sweet, sweet boy!"

My first startled thought was that she was talking to me. Being as how I was right there, and how she'd been looking right at me not a moment before. For all I knew, her interest had been piqued by the idea of my indulging in some kind of behavior so disturbed that it bore discussing with clergy.

"Does it want some sugar, sweetums? Does it need some lovin'?" Sister Tallman added.

I had jumped a little when she first spoke, and now I reckon my eyes were like saucers. Fortunately, before I outright screamed, I realized that Sister Tallman was no longer looking at me. She was looking at something on the floor behind the counter.

I'd never felt such relief.

Reaching down, Sister Tallman picked up a

cat. At least, I think that thing was a cat. It looked like a cat, but it was much bigger than any cat I'd ever seen before.

"Goliath, you sweetheart, come to mama," Sister Tallman was crooning.

I continued to stare. Goliath was appropriately named, all right. Hell, that thing was bigger than some dogs I'd seen. It was bigger than a Maltese, bigger than a toy poodle, bigger than a Lhasa Apso. This mutant had to weigh close to thirty pounds.

This Jackie Gleason of cats had apparently walked up while Brother Tallman was talking. Solid white except for two light gray spots between his ears that made him look as if he were wearing a toupee, this cat looked like a dog dressed in a cat suit. I remembered now hearing about Sister Tallman's cat around town, but this was the first time I'd ever seen it with my own eyes. Up to now, I'd thought folks around Pigeon Fork were exaggerating.

Word was, a couple months ago when a radio station in Louisville had staged a contest to look for the largest cat in Kentucky, Sister Tallman had driven all the way to Louisville to enter hers. When she'd showed up lugging Goliath, other contestants standing there waiting to have their cats weighed had left. Goliath had not won the $5,000 first prize—he'd been beat out by a cat that was a couple ounces heavier—but he'd come close. I'd also heard that the cat that won was grossly obese, whereas it was clear, as I stood there, still pretty much gawking, that Goliath was just one extremely large animal of the feline persuasion. To be totally honest, Goliath was a little on the plump side, but even if he weren't, his frame alone would've still made him huge.

"Goliath, you sweetums," Sister Tallman continued to croon, "you adorable little baby . . ."

I hated to break it to her, but *little* was not a word I'd ever use to describe old Goliath.

A glance toward Brother Tallman made me realize that he might never use the word *adorable* either. His nostrils were flaring up a storm as he watched his wife fawn over Goliath. He noticed me looking at him, though, cleared his throat, and said abruptly, "OK, then. Come on."

Sister Tallman was saying, "Sweet baby, yes, yes, sweet, sweet baby," and scratching Goliath right on his little gray toupee as I followed Brother Tallman into his office. His eyes as sleepy as those of Sister Dank, Goliath, for his part, was purring so loud that I could hear the rumbling all the way down the hall.

"Boy, that's a big cat," I said as I went through the door.

Brother Tallman did roll his eyes this time.

"Sister Tallman sure does seem to be crazy about him," I said.

I was just making conversation, I didn't

mean anything by it. Brother Tallman's nostrils, however, clearly said that I'd broached a sore subject. "Crazy is the word, all right," he said, his tone beleaguered. "Sister Tallman is nuts about that cat. Sometimes, I think she likes that dumb animal better than—" The reverend broke off here, realizing, no doubt, that he was saying more than he intended.

I just looked at him. It would be kinda bad, I reckon, to be losing out to a cat. Even one that was almost your size.

The reverend cleared his throat, reached over, and opened the top right-hand drawer of his desk. Right on top was a navy blue ledger. "Here's the church checkbook." He took it out and handed it to me.

I took it, but I didn't even look through it right away. Something else had struck me right off the bat. "Brother Tallman, this drawer isn't even locked. Is the door to your office locked?" I glanced back at the door we'd come through. It was standing slightly ajar.

Brother Tallman had already been looking annoyed, after confessing that a cat had been beating his time with his own wife. Now he looked downright angry. Nostrils flaring, he snapped, "Of course it's not locked." His tone questioned my intelligence. "Brother Blevins, this is a *church*."

I believe I'd heard this little revelation before. Brother Tallman hurried on, looking angrier by the minute. "There's no reason to lock out the members of my flock. Because all of them—all of them, Brother—are children of the Lord!"

Oh God. The reverend was singsonging again. I started looking through the checkbook. There wasn't much to see, check stub after check stub after check stub for the checks I'd already glanced through back at my office. I turned toward the back, where the deposit slips were attached.

It didn't take a detective to see that quite a few deposit tickets were missing. "Did you use all these deposit tickets yourself?"

The reverend's nostrils were all but flapping in the breeze. "Of course not," he snapped again. "Someone has obviously come in here and taken these slips."

"But it could not have been a church member," I put in.

The reverend's nostrils were going to town. "What did I say? Of course it wasn't a member of my church." Leaning forward, Brother Tallman pointed his finger at me, to emphasize what he was saying.

I hate it when somebody starts pointing at me. It always makes me want to bite the offending finger.

"It was a stranger," Brother Tallman said. "A stranger who came in here and took these deposit tickets. It would've been easy to do."

I had to agree. Since the desk wasn't locked, and the office wasn't locked, it would have been pretty easy. Provided the stranger knew somehow exactly where Brother Tallman kept his checkbook. Of course, maybe the stranger had simply searched the desk until he'd found it. The ledger had been lying right on top in the top drawer.

"Look, Haskell, who you ought to be talking to is—"

At this moment, there was a quick tap on the door. Sister Dank stuck her head in. Her eyes still didn't look sleepy. They looked very alert as they darted in my direction. I believe she was hoping that she'd hear some juicy tidbit of whatever it was that I had to confess. "You two, uh, didn't close the door all the way, so I thought that I—"

Brother Tallman nodded and waved her away. "Sure, sure, close it, OK?"

Sister Dank gave me one more look, and then she somewhat reluctantly pulled the door closed.

I couldn't help but sigh. "You know, Brother Tallman, she thinks I'm in here confessing to something awful, thanks to you," I said. "It's gonna be all over town."

Brother Tallman had the gall to look blank. He looked first at me, then over at the closed door, and then back at me again. Waving his hand in the air, as if dismissing the whole thing as too trivial to discuss, he said, "I'll take care of it, OK? It'll be fine." Brother Tallman cleared his throat. "Like I was saying, you need to do some snooping at the bank branch in E-town," he grumbled. "You don't need to be wasting my money, trying to pin this on one of my flock. You should be going to E-town, and finding out exactly what this thief looked like!"

I just looked at him. Thanks so much for the tip, Brother. It was, no doubt, divinely inspired.

5
$

Shortly after Brother Tallman suggested it, I found myself walking into the E-town branch of Crayton County Federal Bank. Once I left the Pentecostal Church, it only took me about twenty minutes to drive north on Interstate 65 to the Elizabethtown exit, and another ten minutes or so to get to the bank.

I reckon, technically, Elizabethtown would be called a small town. It only has 20,000 people, if you could believe the small sign I passed as I approached the center of town. Compared to Pigeon Fork, however, Elizabethtown is a bustling metropolis. For one thing, E-town— as the locals all call it—has actual fast food, like Wendy's and McDonald's and Pizza Hut. It was rumored a few years back that Pigeon Fork was actually in the running to get a Mickey D's—until the folks from McDonald's

did what they call a market survey. And the
whole McDonald's idea died a quick and terrible death. The way I heard it, the market survey told them loud and clear that there simply
weren't enough folks in the immediate area to
keep a McDonald's going. Now every time I
pass the McDonald's in E-town, I'm impressed.

Once I'd passed the McDonald's, it was only
a few miles down the road to the bank. Actually, it was not exactly a bank. It was the Winn
Dixie Supermarket. That's where the Elizabethtown branch of the Crayton County Bank
is located these days—a few feet to the left of
the checkout counters, and a few feet to the
right of the lettuce and cabbage. I know having your bank right where you do your grocery
shopping is supposed to be real convenient
and all. And I certainly agree. What with the
cost of groceries and household goods these
days, I've always thought that I ought to
mosey on in and just hand over my paycheck
to the supermarket anyway, more or less skip-
ping the middleman. So this sure feels right.

As an ex-cop, though, I can't help but wonder if maybe all this isn't just a little too convenient. If somebody had a mind to, he could
walk in here and stick up a bank and a supermarket all at once. One-stop robbing. The
mega-markets that are springing up all over
really give me pause. There's a MegaMart
that's just opened up here in E-town where

you can go in, buy yourself a gun, a ski mask, and a duffel bag. On your way out, fully equipped with your new purchases, you could hit the MegaMart, a McDonald's, a pharmacy, and a branch bank all located just inside the MegaMart entrance, without having to put a single extra mile on your getaway car.

Talk about convenience.

I don't get into E-town all that often, and I hardly ever go into the MegaMart, so maybe that's why all this convenience still seems a little strange to me. I don't know, but it seems downright peculiar to be walking up to a bank teller's window while overhead the loudspeaker is announcing, "Today's special is lettuce." This is what was being said as I walked through the automatic grocery door, heading toward the bank counter. It took me a moment to realize that the lettuce being referred to was the vegetable.

By the time I walked through the front door of the Winn Dixie, after the trip to the Pentecostal Church and the drive to E-town, it was close to four. The grocery appeared to be full of folks who'd just gotten off work at 3:30 and were picking up a few things on the way home. The bank part of the grocery, however, was empty. Or, rather, the part of the floor directly in front of the bank window.

I wasn't exactly shocked to find no one standing in line. Maybe in the city, having your bank in your grocery is old hat, but out here in the country, it's a brand-new concept. Folks are pretty much set in their ways, too. Around these parts, it takes a while for folks to warm up to a newfangled way of doing things. I'd actually heard two women arguing in Elmo's Drugstore recently—it had been when I was working on yet another big case, this one filled with multivitamins—and apparently, the disagreement had been about whether banks in groceries were "real" banks. One of the women had worried out loud that the grocery bank might lose her money, carting it in the grocery cart from the grocery to the bank.

Judging from that little conversation alone, I'd say that the whole grocery bank concept was going to be a hard sell in small-town America.

I went past the checkout counters and headed straight for the counter beneath the large red, white, and blue sign that said Crayton County Bank. Crayton County Bank recently changed its corporate colors. It used to be a staid gray and burgundy. Now its sign sported a U.S. flag and patriotic colors. I believe the impression they were now trying to give was that it would be un-American not to bank with them.

There was only one teller window open, and only one teller on duty. She was standing with her back to me when I walked up, and for a second there, my heart speeded up some. The woman had pale blond, shoulder-length hair that curled under at the ends, and she was wearing a body-hugging bright red knit dress. From where I was standing, it looked as if that particular body richly deserved hugging, too, going in and out at all the right places.

My mouth actually went dry.

Because, of course, for a moment there, I thought the woman standing in front of me might actually be my ex-wife Claudine. That's her real name. I usually call her by the pet name I've got for her—*Claudzilla*. Mainly because, during our five years of wedded lack-of-bliss, that woman went through my charge cards and my savings account much like Godzilla went through New York.

My heart had picked up considerable speed by the time the teller finally turned around. I will admit that at one time the sight of Claudzilla made my heart race for an entirely different reason, but today when I run into her and my heart starts going like a trip-hammer, it can only mean one thing.

Fear.

Lord, that woman is one scary human being.

Thank God when the teller turned around, she didn't look the least bit like Claudzilla. She had a long horse face, a large nose, and horn-rimmed glasses. The only thing she seemed to have in common with Claudzilla was her figure. I actually felt a wave of relief looking at the teller's unattractive face. It wasn't just relief that I wasn't going to have to have a conversation with Claudzilla, it was also relief that Claudzilla was not working in a bank, of all places. Frankly, the idea of Claudzilla actually handling large sums of money on a daily basis was pretty appalling. Talk about putting a fox in charge of the chickens.

The small ceramic sign to the right of the teller window told me that the teller's name was Janice Wendell. Next to the ceramic sign, there was a matching ceramic picture frame. You see a lot of these photos in banks around these parts. Most of the pictures feature the teller's family—the spouse and the children. I believe the thinking behind this is that, seeing these photos, the customer is supposed to have an immediate rapport with the person behind the counter. In an instant, you not only know this person, you also know her family.

Then, too, I believe the photo display might also be a little preventive medicine. If the person approaching the teller happens to have it in his mind to rob the place and possibly shoot the teller, he might be dissuaded knowing there's a family somewhere who'd be left without a mom or a dad. I stared at Janice's photo. It showed her sitting stiffly in a Queen Anne chair with a large German shepherd at her side and a Siamese cat on her lap. The dog appeared to be eyeing the cat hungrily. Evidently, the message here was that if something happened to Janice, the cat was a goner.

"May I help you?" Janice said with a practiced smile.

I returned her smile. "You sure can. I want to make a deposit." I handed her the deposit ticket that the reverend had given me, and a hundred-dollar bill. Hey, I would've deposited more, but that's all Brother Tallman would give me. I wasn't about to deposit my own money. The good reverend would, no doubt, decide that God had touched me, much like He'd touched whoever it was who'd made the original deposits, and that, since it was God's will, Brother Tallman would have no qualms about keeping every cent of my money.

"Okey-dokey," Janice said. She made it sound as if this was the best idea she'd heard all day. She started doing whatever tellers do, tapping keys and stamping the back of the deposit ticket.

"I'll be making the deposit from now on," I said. I watched her face for a reaction.

She didn't disappoint me. She stopped looking at what she was doing and looked up at me, her eyes widening behind the horn-rims. "Oh? What happened to the reverend?"

I blinked a couple times at that one. Then I swallowed hard and tried to keep my face perfectly still. So as not to betray the fact that this was something of a surprise. "The reverend?"

She shrugged. "Oh. Well. Maybe he isn't a reverend. That's just what me and Lavinia call him. Lavinia Doss is the other teller who works here. She and I just guessed that he had to be a preacher. On account of him making deposits into a church bank account."

I nodded. Made sense to me.

"And on account of how he talked, you know."

I tried to look pretty disinterested. I also tried to sound real casual. "Oh? How did he talk?"

She went back to doing the bank teller thing, her eyes now on her computer screen. "Well, you know. Just like a preacher. You know how they do? With that kinda singsongy way of talking, you know?"

Oh yeah, I knew, all right. I cleared my throat and stretched my mouth into a smile. "That sure sounds like our preacher all right. I'm running errands for him these days. He wore black all the time, right?"

Janice had been starting to look at me a little funny, like maybe she was beginning to wonder—since I was asking so many questions—if maybe I didn't really know the guy she'd been describing at all. When I said this last, though, she gave me a real big grin and looked a little relieved. "That's right! He *always* wears black. Black shirt, black pants, black everything. Even his hat."

I was having a real hard time holding my face perfectly still. If that wasn't Reverend Tallman, I'd eat his hat. So what was going on here? If he was making deposits himself, where was he getting all the money to deposit? And why would he ask me to look into it if all I was going to find out was what he already knew?

Janice was back to tapping keys. "Even his beard is black. Well, it's almost black. Real dark brown, anyway."

That one took me by surprise. "His beard?"

Janice was waiting for the machine she'd been tapping to print out my deposit slip. "He still has the beard, doesn't he?" Janice glanced over at her machine, and then back at me. "When the reverend first came in here, I thought his beard sort of looked like Harrison Ford's. You know, the way Harrison Ford's beard looked at the beginning of that Fugitive movie? Only, I guess, a little thicker. You know? I sure hope the reverend hasn't shaved off that nice beard."

I just looked at her. "You know" must've been one of Janice's favorite phrases. The trouble was, I didn't know. None of what she was telling me made any sense. Did Brother Tallman really think that wearing a fake beard was all the disguise he needed? Was he kidding? Did he think he could wear the same clothes he always wore, and even the same hat? And he could even talk the way he does, and nobody would make the connection? Did he really believe that all he had to do was put on a beard and nobody would guess who he really was?

Or was somebody else making deposits into the church account, deliberately dressing like the reverend and sounding like the reverend, just so if anybody came along, asking questions, it would simply be assumed that the Phantom Depositor was indeed the reverend. Wearing a disguise that wasn't a disguise at all. When you come right down to it, it would not be all that hard a thing to do to sound like Brother Tall-man either. You might have to listen to a few Jerry Falwell sermons—but after a while, you'd have the whole singsong voice inflection thing down.

When the reverend first told me about the huge deposits, and the sudden withdrawal, it had occurred to me right away, of course, that somebody might be using the Pentecostal Church account in a money laundering scheme. What could be a better cover than a church? That amount of money could easily be the profits from selling marijuana, or other drugs, or just about anything illegal. In the remote countryside around Pigeon Fork, I had no doubt that there were quite a few folks who'd decided to make pot one of their cash crops. Fact is, I believe I'd read somewhere recently that pot is second only to tobacco as Kentucky's largest cash crop, so I reckon I'd be fooling myself if I thought that such business ventures did not exist anywhere around these parts. After all, in the time I'd been back in town, I'd even helped bring a couple pot growers to justice. Just because those two were in jail, though, didn't mean there weren't others.

If somebody selling drugs or other illegal items had sold them to someone suspicious—someone who was suspected of somehow marking the bills used in the payoff—then making use of the church account to launder the money would be perfect. When you withdrew the money, you'd get nice, clean, unmarked bills from Crayton Federal's vaults.

And yet, wasn't all this a little bit farfetched? In the eight years I spent as a cop, I'd found out that in ninety-nine percent of the cases, the simplest explanation turns out to be the right one. In this case, the simplest explanation was that Brother Tallman was making the deposits himself. And yet, the questions remained: Where was he getting all that money? And why would he hire me to investigate?

I wished I had brought along a photo of Brother Tallman so I could be a little more positive that the good reverend was really not trying to pull a fast one. It would certainly relieve my mind. Not that I'd ever believe that a man of God would ever be guilty of anything unseemly. Oh no. I mean, ask Jim Bakker. Or Jimmy Swaggart.

Although it would've been a real good idea, it sure would've been difficult to ask Brother Tallman for a photograph. I mean, just how would you put that? *Oh, by the way, Brother Tallman, just in case you're lying through your teeth, could I have a photograph of you to verify what you're telling me? To show the teller at the bank, so she could tell me that it was really not you who has been making the deposits?* Of course, that right there could be the reason for the beard. Would Janice here be able to make a positive ID if she saw a photo of a clean-shaven Brother Tallman?

Janice was staring back at me, waiting for me to tell her if the reverend still had a beard. I wasn't sure what to say. I decided to go, however, with what might make things more difficult for the Phantom Depositor. The truth. "Yeah, well, I'm afraid the reverend doesn't have a beard."

Janice blinked behind her horn-rims. "My goodness, he must've shaved it awful quick. I mean, he was just in here yesterday, you know, making another withdrawal."

It was my turn to blink. Another withdrawal? Brother Tallman was not going to be happy to hear about this. It was suddenly looking like an awful good thing that I got my money up front. "A withdrawal, huh?" I hoped I sounded casual. "Don't suppose you'd tell me how much of a withdrawal was made, would you?"

Janice's reaction was not quite what I hoped. She actually snickered, like she thought that I was surely joking. "Oh, I couldn't do that. This isn't your account, you know."

"You wouldn't give me the current balance then, either?"

Janice just grinned this time, which I must admit was a big improvement over the snickering. "I couldn't possibly. That kind of information is only given to the current account holder."

She sounded as if she were reciting from the bank's employee manual.

The machine on Janice's desk was kicking out my deposit slip. Janice handed me the thing and gave me another practiced smile. "Thank you for banking with Crayton Federal," she said. I was pretty sure that this parting phrase was in the manual, too.

I knew her saying that was supposed to send me on my merry way, but I wasn't ready to leave yet. If the deposits were not profits from some illegal shenanigans, then there was another possibility that had occurred to me. "You know," I began. When in Rome, you talk like the Romans talk. "I've been thinking."

Janice had dismissed me, and she started to turn around again. I could see now what she'd been doing before I came up. On top of the desk in back of her was a romance novel. It was one of those with Fabio on the front. He stood at the prow of a ship, with a sword in one hand, a scantily clad woman in the other, and he didn't even seem close to losing his balance. His long hair was blowing in the breeze as usual. And, even though it looked as if he was in the middle of the ocean, and it was obviously pretty windy, Fabio wasn't wearing a shirt. He didn't even look cold. Whatta man.

Janice reluctantly turned her attention back to me. "The reverend has been making an awful lot of deposits," I said, "into our church account. They've all been in cash, right?" This was an outright guess, but Janice's quick nod confirmed that I was right. "Well, you know, being a man of God, the reverend is awful trusting. Do you know if anybody has tested the money? To make absolutely certain that it's not counterfeit?"

Janice didn't take that little question well. She drew herself up a little taller, and as she spoke, two bright spots of color appeared on each cheek. "Look, we're a real bank. Understand? I'm getting sick and tired of people coming up to me and asking if this is a real bank. It's real, OK? And, of course, we test large deposits of cash to make sure they aren't counterfeit. It's standard procedure. For *banks.*"

OK, so Janice was a little touchy. I guess being a bank in the middle of a grocery in the middle of Small Town USA had not exactly been a cakewalk. I tried to mend the damage. "Look, I didn't mean anything. I was just asking—"

"I mean, we may be a bank branch in a grocery but, by God, we're up on all the latest, you know." Janice now sounded more than a little touchy. She sounded irritated. "We look at the bills under an ultraviolet light and magnification. Money is printed on pretty special paper, you know. The kind that's pretty hard to fake because it has these fine red and blue threads embedded in it, and there's type on bills that's all but invisible to the naked eye, you know."

In this case, of course, I did know. As an ex-cop, I was well aware of the differences between genuine currency and counterfeit. There were quite a few things you looked for. Like on a genuine bill, the sawtooth points of the Federal Reserve and Treasury seals are clear, distinct, and sharp. The seals on counterfeit bills may have uneven, blunt, or broken sawtooth points. The background of the portrait is often too dark and mottled. On genuine bills, serial numbers are printed in the same color as the Treasury seal. On a counterfeit, the serial number may differ in color or shade of ink from the Treasury seal. The tiny, fine lines in the border of a genuine bill are clear and unbroken. On the counterfeit, the lines in the outer margin and scrollwork may be blurred and fuzzy. It's stuff like this that you look for.

Janice's eyes were shooting sparks behind her horn-rims, but I ignored them. "Did you ever rub the bills on a piece of paper to see if they would smear?"

Janice's mouth tightened. "Of course we didn't do that. Because it wouldn't matter if the bills smeared or not. Some folks believe that if the ink rubs off, it's gotta be counterfeit, but that's not true. The real stuff can leave ink smears, too, when you rub it on paper."

OK, I admit it. I was just testing her. Just trying to see how much she really did know about counterfeit money.

"Thanks for banking with Crayton County Federal," Janice added. The phrase, oddly enough, didn't sound quite as friendly as before. She started to turn her attention back to Fabio, but once again, I interrupted.

"I was just wondering, that's all. I mean, since the deposits are mostly in the newly issued currency, I know it's harder to detect counterfeit bills."

Janice just looked at me for a moment. "I think you know very well that the new bills have added security features that make counterfeit currency *easier* to detect. Not harder."

I did, in fact, know this. I was just testing her once again. The new currency has a clear, inscribed thread incorporated into the paper that runs vertically through the clear field to the left of the Federal Reserve seal on all notes except the dollar denomination. Printed on the thread is a denomination identifier. For example, on the twenty-dollar bill, "USA TWENTY USA TWENTY" is repeated along the entire length of the thread. The thread and the printing can only be seen by holding the note up to a light.

"Besides, it doesn't matter what the new currency is like, because the deposits have all been made in older currency." Janice was now leaning forward, her eyes fixed on my face. As if maybe she was trying to commit my features to memory. "So why are you asking so many questions about counterfeit money, huh?" She had not yet closed her cash drawer, and she reached in and retrieved the hundred-dollar bill I'd just deposited. She snapped on a lamp that was sitting on her desk, and she held the bill under the light. She stared at the bill for a second, then picked it up to peer at it closely, and then stuck it under the light again.

It took me a moment to realize what she was doing. She was making sure that the bill I'd given her was real. Old Janice here actually thought I could be trying to pass counterfeit money.

A thing like this could really hurt your feelings.

Not to mention, did she really think I'd be

asking about counterfeit money if I'd actually been a counterfeiter?

Apparently, the bill passed muster, because Janice returned it to her cash drawer. She looked a little disappointed. Apparently, the sight of me being hauled off in handcuffs would've brightened her day. "Thank you for banking with Crayton County Federal," she said sulkily.

"You're welcome," I said, and smiled at her.

Janice did not return my smile.

So much for customer service.

6
§

Funniest thing, the drive back from Elizabethtown seemed to take a lot longer than the
drive there. I reckon it was on account of my
being a tad overanxious to have me a little
chat with Brother Tallman about what I'd
just learned from Janice at the grocery bank.
Call me sensitive, but if the good reverend
was truly trying to pull a fast one having me
investigate bank deposits that he himself was
making, I was real interested in discussing
that with him. I was also real curious as to
how Brother Tallman had come into all the
money he was depositing. There was enough
cop still left in me to need an answer to that
little question.

What's more, if the good reverend tried to
tell me again that the money had been a gift
from God, then I believed I'd have to ask him

this time exactly where God had gotten all that cash.

The drive back to the Pentecostal Church of the Holy Scriptures took me right past the exit off Interstate 65 that eventually led to my house, but I didn't even consider stopping by home. I was that anxious to talk to the reverend. If I were a nicer person, though, I would have stopped. You see, my dog Rip has a little problem that he has had ever since I brought him home as a puppy. Of course, when he was a puppy, his problem was kind of cute.

Rip, you see, is psychologically disturbed. At least, that's what I say when I'm in a good mood. When I'm in a bad mood, I say Rip is mentally deranged. I'm not sure what happened to him to get him this way, but can you believe, Rip is terrified of going up and down stairs? I mean, shaking, whimpering, slobbering terrified.

It wouldn't be so bad, I guess, except that he and I happen to live in an A-frame on top of a hill, with a deck all the way around it. So the only way Rip can get to the side yard where he does his business is to go downstairs. I've tried dragging that dog downstairs by his collar, I've tried coaxing him downstairs with pieces of sirloin, I've tried pushing him downstairs from behind, but nothing has worked. Except, of course, for one thing. *Carrying* him downstairs. That one works. Every damn time. Amazingly enough.

Back when Rip was a puppy, like I said, it was kind of cute having to carry this squirming little ball of fluff out to the side yard. Of course, back when I first got Rip, I'd already lost two puppies. I wasn't sure what was killing them. I'm still not. I'd get them their shots, have them checked out by the vet, and in no time at all, they'd have something fatal. Fact is, that's why I called Rip what I did in the first place. I was so sure that this new puppy was going to go the way of the other two that I just painted R.I.P. on his doghouse.

I reckon I was so glad Rip didn't immediately start dying that it didn't even occur to me that carrying Rip out to the side yard might get to be a real nuisance after a while. I was pretty much convinced that Rip himself wouldn't be here after a while, so it wasn't going to be a problem. In fact, for the longest time, I didn't even *try* to get him to change his furry mind about stairs. I was that sure that Rip was going to have himself a short life.

Rip, however, not only did not have a short life, he positively thrived. Today that dumb dog has got to weigh at least seventy pounds. Of course, I should not be surprised that he's big. His mom, Princess, was a full-blooded German shepherd, and his dad was a large black mongrel capable of jumping a seven-foot-high fence. This last I have on good authority from Princess's owner. The owner had been intending to breed Princess the very next day to another purebred German shepherd and instead ended up with twelve mixed puppies and Princess with a smile on her furry face.

Knowing all this, I reckon I should be glad Rip isn't any bigger than he is. Because hauling his big butt out to the yard, while he happily tries to lick my ears, takes some doing. What's more, I do it at least twice a day, to make sure old Rip doesn't leave me a doggie memento on my deck.

Like I said, on my way back from E-town, I probably should've stopped and given Rip a quick trip to the side yard. I thought, though, that he could probably hold it another couple hours or so. Not to mention, maybe if he got uncomfortable enough—and having learned through experience that if he does anything whatsoever on my deck, he was going to have a close encounter with a rolled-up newspaper—old Rip might actually give going downstairs a whirl.

Once I passed the exit off the interstate that led to my house, it was only about twenty more minutes, and I was once again pulling into the parking lot out in front of the Pentecostal Church. It was starting to get dark, but the lights were still on inside. The church van and the Tercel were still in the parking lot out front, but Sister Tallman's Aspire was nowhere to be seen. I parked my truck and headed inside.

This time when I went into the office, there was no one behind the counter. I could hear voices, though, coming from the direction of Brother Tallman's private office. I went around the counter and headed that way. The door wasn't standing wide open, but it wasn't exactly shut, either. It stood just slightly ajar, as if maybe somebody had tried to close it, and when it hadn't shut all the way, they hadn't noticed.

Since the door was open still, I could hear every word that was being said inside. "It's just terrible. I feel so weak. I just can't seem to resist temptation." This was Sister Dank's voice. It sounded a little muffled, but it was clearly her voice.

"We're all sinners, Sister. We just can't help ourselves." Even though he was not speaking in his distinctive singsong, this was without a doubt Brother Tallman. "It's our curse."

I may have been wrong, but the good reverend did not sound all that unhappy to have to bear up under the particular curse he was discussing.

I stepped closer to the door, and yes—calling upon a tried-and-true professional private eye technique—I peeped through the space between the door and the doorjamb. As luck would have it, Brother Tallman and Sister Dank were standing directly in my line of vision. One look told me why Sister Dank's voice was muffled. Brother Tallman had his arms around her, and her face was more or less buried in his chest. "It's OK," Brother Tallman went on, patting Sister Dank's back. "It's OK."

Sister Dank took a deep breath. "But I ought to be able to resist. I ought to be stronger."

"We can't help being human, Sister," Brother Tallman said.

Sister Dank took a deep breath. "So, do you think she suspects? Do you think she has any idea?"

I actually caught my breath. Good heavens. Could the "she" that Sister Dank mentioned— could that be Sister Tallman? If it was, then what exactly was Sister Tallman supposed to suspect? Was it possible that these two could be having an affair?

I took another long look at Sister Dank. Let me see, huge mass of long brown hair, no makeup, round face, sleepy eyes, and dressed in a shapeless navy blue sweat suit. I could be wrong, but the idea of Sister Dank as a temptress was something of a stretch. Still, there was no accounting for taste. Different strokes for different folks, as they say.

"She has no idea, believe me," Brother Tallman was saying. "It'll come as a complete surprise."

"You really think so?" As she said this, Sister Dank lifted her head to look up at the reverend, and for a moment I actually thought he was going to plant one on her. Really. His face appeared to be moving in her face's direction.

This was not something I wanted to see, believe me. In fact, I was pretty sure I could skip for the rest of my natural life the image of the good reverend and his secretary putting a lip lock on one another, and I would only feel relieved.

Not to mention, I was pretty shocked. I know that sounds downright strange, being as how I've seen and heard quite a few mind-blowing things over the course of my two careers as a cop and a private eye. I've investigated the multiple homicide of a grandmother and her pets. I've gotten to know up close and personal several folks who'd apparently gone through all the possible solutions to a given problem and finally decided on murder as the method of choice. And yet, Sister Dank and Brother Tallman shocked me. Mainly, I reckon, because these two were supposed to be super-duper religious folk. As such, weren't they supposed to be something of an example for the rest of us lowly sinner types?

"She doesn't know a thing," Brother Tallman was saying as I took a deep breath and knocked loudly on the door.

"Brother Tallman?" I called out. "Are you in there?"

Strangely enough, when Brother Tallman opened the door seconds later, Sister Dank was clear across the room, standing over by the reverend's desk. I had to hand it to her. She must've crossed the room in a single bound. Hell, the woman could put Superman to shame.

Brother Tallman had started doing his singsong again. "Brother Blevins! Well, I sure didn't expect to see you again today. Was there something else you wanted to talk about?"

Oh for God's sakes. I'd forgotten I was still undercover. I directed a quick glance toward Sister Dank, just to see how she took the idea of my having yet another horrible deed to confess to clergy.

To my surprise, she was looking straight at me with this odd little smile on her round face. She looked a tad flushed, and I was pretty sure that, even from across the room, I could still see the indentations of buttons on her right cheek, from where her face had been pressed against the good reverend's suit coat. Her manner, however, was clearly not what it had been earlier. Instead of staring at me the way she'd been doing when I'd left—like maybe I'd just crawled out from under a rock—she was now looking at me with a strange sort of smile on her face. Perhaps she thought she and I now had something in common, sinner-types that we were. She nodded at me as she said, "Brother Blevins."

Around these parts, just saying your name is the same as saying hello. Sister Dank's voice, however, had a strange lilt. Like she might actually be *glad* to see me again.

I just stared back at her. I'd just interrupted what had looked to me to be a pretty intimate moment with Brother Tallman, and Sister Dank was looking at me and *smiling*? Was I missing something here?

"I'm sure you'll need some privacy again," Sister Dank went on, still giving me that strange little smile. "So I'll leave you two alone."

Brother Tallman and I watched in silence as Sister Dank walked out of the room. She'd no sooner taken two steps out the door, closing it behind her with a soft click this time, when the good reverend turned to me. "OK, what did you find out?"

I had him sit down at his desk, made myself comfortable in the chair opposite him, and then I laid it all out for him. How the person who had been making the deposits at the bank in E-town had, according to Janice-the-teller's description, looked suspiciously like Brother Tallman himself. How the guy had been dressed in black, how he'd been pretty much the reverend's height and weight. I even told Brother Tallman how the two tellers at the bank always referred to the guy as "The Reverend."

The more I told Brother Tallman, the bigger his eyes got. "Why, Brother Blevins, this is an outrage! You've got to find out who this is!" he finally burst out.

I just looked at him. I thought I already knew who it was.

"I can NOT believe there is somebody running around impersonating me!" Brother Tallman said.

What could I say? Apparently, the good reverend and I agreed on something.

"He even talks like you," I said.

Brother Tallman had apparently calmed down enough to pick up on my general attitude of unbridled skepticism. His eyes narrowed a tad as he stared back at me. He cleared his throat and said, "You know, learning to talk like me wouldn't be all that hard. I mean, all you'd have to do is watch any one of a dozen evangelist shows on cable television— or on satellite. They all sound just like me, when they're delivering God's message. If you listened, you could pick it up in no time."

He made it sound as if evangelism was an American dialect. Like Cajun. Of course, now that I thought about it, maybe he was right.

Brother Tallman was running his hand through his hair and looking rattled. "There aren't as many TV evangelists as there used to be, and that's a real shame. But there's still quite a few left, singing His praises. Ministering to the faithful. Doing the Lord's work."

"Asking folks to spend ten dollars for a fake gold necklace with a cross dangling from it that isn't worth a buck ninety-nine," I added.

I hadn't meant to say that. It just sort of slipped out. I reckon seeing the reverend with his arms around Sister Dank had put me in a real bad mood. I mean, the word *hypocrite* did spring to mind. Hearing him going on about TV evangelists also made me remember how my mom, during the last year of her life, when she'd been suffering pretty bad with cancer, had spent quite a chunk of change, sending away for necklaces and crosses and the like, in the hopes that one of them would work a miracle for her. It had been a real sad thing to watch.

Brother Tallman was now looking downright sad himself. He looked at me with pity in his eyes. "It's not the necklace that folks are paying for, Brother Blevins. It's the blessing that comes with the necklace. The *blessing*, do you understand? Sometimes, folks need that kind of comfort."

I just looked at him. "Yeah, well, sometimes, folks just need their ten dollars."

Brother Tallman frowned at me, and since he was frowning anyway, I thought I might as well tell him the rest of it. "The teller at the bank also told me something else. There's been another withdrawal."

Brother Tallman's reaction was pretty predictable. He audibly gasped, and then he yelled, "Oh dear God in heaven! Oh dear God in heaven!"

"You might want to check your balance. They wouldn't give it to me."

Brother Tallman glanced at his watch. "Oh dear God in heaven!"

I was getting a little tired of hearing him say that.

"Brother Blevins," the reverend went on, "the bank is closed now. It's closed, do you hear? I won't be able to find anything out tonight. And tomorrow is Thursday!"

He didn't have to say anything else. I knew what he meant. In Pigeon Fork, Thursdays are to local banks what Thursdays are to doctors in the rest of America. On Thursday, all the local banks in Pigeon Fork are closed, and like doctors, banks are not about to make house calls.

The banks in Pigeon Fork have been doing it this way for years, but I don't quite understand why they haven't changed with the times. You'd think that nowadays when national banks were all working real hard to be more convenient—installing anytime teller machines, automating customer service on the phone so that you could dial up your account information any old time you wanted, and even putting up Web sites—the local banks would be falling all over themselves trying to outshine the competition.

That sure isn't the case, though. Pigeon Fork only has two local banks—Crayton County Federal and Peoples Savings Bank of Crayton County—and the two of them seem to be locked in a contest as to who could be the most difficult to do business with. The Crayton County Federal branch seemed to be winning lately, offering banking hours from 8 to 3 on Monday, 9 to 4 on Tuesday, 2 to 4 on Wednesday, closing completely on Thursday, and opening again from 3 to 7 on Friday. You needed a scorecard to figure out when the hell they were open. Neither bank offered automated anything, be it customer service by phone or an ATM. If you wanted information on your account, you were going to have to talk to an actual human being. If you wanted to make a withdrawal, that human being—likely as not—would be rude.

"I'm going to have to drive all the way to E-town to find out how much is left in my account," Brother Tallman was whining.

I tried to look sympathetic, but I still wasn't totally convinced that Brother Tallman didn't already know the exact balance on his account. Oh, the good reverend looked genuinely upset and all, but for all I knew, he was just one helluva good actor.

Brother Tallman must've picked up on what

was going through my mind. He ran his hand through his hair, and then he said, "Look, why would I need to wear a beard if I was impersonating myself?"

It was a good question. I had an equally good answer, though. "So people would think you were somebody impersonating you, of course. Without the beard, they'd have known for sure it was you. The tellers at the grocery bank would be able to recognize you. And folks might start asking questions as to where the money had come from, so—"

Brother Tallman interrupted me, frowning big-time now. "Look, would I have hired you if I was the one depositing money into the church account? Would that make sense? If I was guilty, would I want you nosing around?"

I shrugged. "You would, if you thought you could fool me into thinking it was somebody else. You also would want me nosing around if some money had disappeared from your account, and you didn't want to arouse any suspicion looking into it yourself."

Brother Tallman raised his eyes heavenward, as if asking for divine help. "Lord forgive him the sin of suspicion," he said.

I didn't know what to say. Since when had suspicion become a sin?

Dragging his eyes away from heaven and back to me, Brother Tallman said, "Look, Brother Blevins, it doesn't really matter whether you think I'm guilty or not. I've hired you to do a job, and I want you to get out of here and do it. I want to know who's behind all this mess with the church account, and I want to know fast." He picked up a pencil off his desk and started chewing on the end of it. "Now, if you'll excuse me, I've got a sermon to write for Sunday."

I appeared to be dismissed.

I headed straight out the door and made my way back to the counter out front. I was kind of surprised that Sister Dank was still there, but I figured she might've been waiting until I left she could get herself another hug from the good reverend. And, for all I knew, a lot more.

I gave her a quick nod, intending to sail right out the front door, but Sister Dank actually smiled at me, her sleepy eyes looking a little more alert than usual. "Brother Blevins," she said, "say hi to Imogene for me, OK?"

I stopped and looked at her. "You know Imogene?" I don't know why I was surprised that Sister Dank would know my girlfriend. In a town the size of Pigeon Fork, everybody pretty much knows everybody else. If you don't actually know them, you've heard of them. Then, too, Imogene was a real estate agent, so she got around more than most.

Sister Dank nodded. "Went to school with her. Lovely person. Just lovely. You're a lucky man."

I couldn't argue with that. "Yep, I'm lucky all right."

"I sure hope you two will be very happy," Sister Dank added. Her smile was looking odd again.

"Thanks," I said uneasily, watching Sister Dank pretty closely now. Again I wondered, was there something going on here that I was missing?

"Imogene, as far as I'm concerned, is right up there with Sister Tallman. And Sister Tallman, mind you, is the finest woman I've ever met."

I couldn't help but wonder if Sister Dank suspected that I'd just seen her hugging the husband of the finest woman she'd ever met, and she was now trying to reassure me that nothing whatsoever really was going on. It did seem as good a time as any to find out some more information. "I reckon you've been working here a long time?" I said. "So you know Sister Tallman pretty well?"

"Three years," Sister Dank said. "And I tell you, Sister Tallman is just a saint on earth, that's what she is. A saint. Why, she just can't resist taking in strays. That's how she ended up with Goliath, you know."

I shook my head. "No, I didn't know. Was Goliath a stray?" Somehow, I couldn't quite picture that cat ever not knowing where his next meal was coming from. Goliath sure didn't look as if he'd missed any. Of course, he probably hadn't. If Goliath spotted something he wanted to eat, he probably just ran up and took it. Mice probably just took one look at him and gave themselves up.

Sister Dank nodded, her brown mass of hair bobbing around her head. "Goliath had been given to the pound by his previous owner. Ain't that awful?"

I immediately nodded just so she'd keep talking, but to tell the truth, I wasn't sure how awful it was. I didn't have enough information to make that kind of judgment. I mean, for all I knew, Goliath's previous owner had just gotten tired of fighting with him over whatever food was in the house. Or maybe his owner had gotten home from work one day, and Goliath had consumed everything in the kitchen cabinets, the refrigerator, and he was gnawing on a sofa leg.

All of these, to my way of thinking, were distinct possibilities and might have made Goliath's previous owner a tad anxious to find Goliath other living quarters.

Sister Dank, however, was on a roll. "To just throw away a pet like that." Her voice shook with indignation. "Why, folks who can do that kind of thing to a poor, defenseless animal—"

Here she lost me again. *Goliath?* Defenseless? That cat could take on Hell's Angels and come out ahead.

"—well, they ought to be, they ought to be—"

Sister Dank seemed to be searching for the right word.

"Crucified?" I suggested.

Sister Dank nodded even more vigorously. "You're right, Brother! You're absolutely right! Actually, crucifixion is too good for them. Why, they ought to—"

It looked as if we could be on this subject for a while. Sister Dank's sleepy eyes had opened considerably, and they were bright with glee as she hurried on. "—they ought to feed them to the lions! That's what! They ought to put 'em in an arena, and have lions tear them to itty-bitty—"

Have I mentioned that members of the Pentecostal Church seem to relish the idea of inflicting punishment on the rest of mankind? Before Sister Dank started going into graphic detail regarding the appropriateness of serving people up as lion lunch, I interrupted. "So, Sister Tallman found Goliath at the pound, huh?"

Sister Dank looked a little dismayed to be interrupted while she was so cheerfully envisioning the horrible death of a fellow human being, but she allowed me to change the subject anyway. "Yep, they did a special one day on WHAS." I nodded. WHAS is a television station in Louisville. "It was about all the animals at the pound in Louisville that had to be put to sleep every day because nobody would give them a home. And, well, Sister Tallman's got such a big heart that she got in her car right that minute and drove all the way to Louisville to save one of them animal's lives." Sister Dank took a deep breath, apparently gearing up for a big finish. "That animal was Goliath."

She made it sound as if maybe Goliath had turned out to be the Thomas Edison of cats. That, perhaps, he'd gone on from humble beginnings to world acclaim as the inventor of electric catnip or something.

"No kidding," I said. "She adopted Goliath, huh?"

Sister Dank nodded. "No kidding," she said.

Having said, "No kidding" once, I wasn't sure what to say next. "Wow," was all I could come up with.

Sister Dank nodded again, patting at her brown hair. "Then there's her charity work."

"Charity?" In Pigeon Fork, there aren't a lot of charities to speak of. I reckon the number of charities in any town is directly proportional to the number of folks in the vicinity. In a town the size of Pigeon Fork, there was every possibility that the number of charities was in the minus.

"Oh my yes, she's real busy. She does volunteer work all the time—you know, reading to the kids at the elementary school, helping out the women's club with their clothing drive, visiting the prison, serving food at the soup kitchen."

I held up my hand. OK. I knew Pigeon Fork had an elementary school, and a soup kitchen, and a women's club. But a *prison*? The only way Pigeon Fork could have anything even close to a prison was if every family in town kept a convict in their home. Shackled to the refrigerator, or something like that. Somehow, I think if that were the case, I'd have heard about it by now. "Where does Sister Tallman do her prison work?"

Sister Dank shrugged "Oh, she drives to Eddyville two or three times a week."

I blinked at that one. Eddyville was a small town of about 20,000 with the proud distinction of being home to the only maximum security prison in Kentucky. It was roughly a three-hour drive from Pigeon Fork.

"Fact is, Sister Tallman was so good at visiting and such," Sister Dank went on, "that they made her a spiritual advisor to one of the prisoners there."

I tried to look impressed. "Really? You don't happen to know the name of that prisoner, do you?"

Sister Dank wrinkled her nose as she thought. "Bailey," she finally said. "Bailey Prather. Sister Tallman used to talk about him quite a bit when she first started visiting out there about seven or eight months ago. That poor, poor man. From what I heard, his soul needed saving bad."

I'd just bet it did. "What was he doing time for?"

"Robbery. He stole a whole lot of money from a credit union."

If I'd been a dog, my ears would've pricked up. *A whole lot of money?* Could it be something like a quarter of a million dollars by any chance?

I could have been leaping to some pretty far-fetched conclusions, but let's face it, it wouldn't be the first time that a very nice woman started out trying to do a good deed and ended up being used. It sure seemed to me as if I ought to have me a little talk with the infamous Bailey Prather.

7
§

I would've liked to have stayed a little longer and asked Sister Dank a few more questions, but I was beginning to hear Rip's whimpering in my head. That dog, I might as well admit, has me well trained. He's taught me to fetch—that is, to fetch him food from the kitchen. He's taught me to sit—to sit and pet him. And he's also taught me to come—to come quickly if I don't want to have to hose off my deck. Like the obedient animal that I am, I immediately cut short the conversation with the good sister by saying, "Well, I reckon I'd best be heading on home."

This, for some reason, encouraged Sister Dank to say, "Well, I'm real glad that we got to talk, Brother Blevins. You tell Imogene how happy I am about you and her, OK?" Her sleepy eyes got even more sleepy-looking as she grinned at me. "And let me be the first to congratulate you."

I said what I always say when I'm being congratulated about something: "Thanks." And I headed out the door.

On the way home, bouncing down winding country roads in my pickup, I didn't give a second thought to what Sister Dank had just said. At least, I didn't until I was almost home. I reckon all my brain cells were pretty much taken up with Sister Tallman and her frequent trips to Eddyville. And wondering about a certain prisoner named Bailey Prather.

As luck would have it, I had me a friend who had a cousin who worked at Eddyville. This friend of mine, who shall remain nameless, had been with the Louisville Police Department since before I signed on, and he owed me one. Actually, since I'd covered his butt about a million times over the course of my illustrious eight-year career with the department, Nameless owed me a lot more than one.

By the time I was turning onto the gravel road that led to my driveway, I'd decided that I was going to give Nameless a call as soon as I walked in my front door. If I remembered correctly, Nameless's cousin was pretty high up in what Nameless used to refer to as "the toilet chain of command" at Eddyville Prison. I sure wanted to hear anything Nameless or his cousin could find out about the infamous Bailey Prather.

I turned into my driveway, stopped my truck briefly to put it into its lowest gear, and began the steep climb to the top. My driveway is not only extremely steep, it's also far, far too long. About a quarter of a mile, in fact. It's so long and steep that Jehovah's Witnesses don't even bother to come up—they just leave me their pamphlets in my mailbox.

If we don't get Jehovah's Witnesses dropping by, then I reckon it goes without saying that Rip and I don't get many visitors at all. The A-frame we live in not only sits at the top of a steep hill, it also sits smack-dab in the middle of five wooded acres. Personally, I really like the seclusion. I can't say that Rip likes it, though, because with nobody dropping by, he doesn't get to try out his bark too often. I suppose that's why that dumb dog has apparently made up his mind that, since he almost never gets the chance to growl and snarl and bark at strangers, he's going to have to make up for lost time whenever I show up.

I was only halfway up my hill, and already I could hear Rip doing his routine up there. It sounded like maybe there was a pack of dogs up at the top of the hill and every one of them had been driven mad with rage. What can I say? That dog sure does know how to enjoy himself.

I was thinking about Rip, and wondering

about his sanity, when it hit me. I reckon it was the idea of sanity—or a lack thereof—that made the connection in my mind.

Sister Dank had *congratulated* me and Imogene. Just as if she'd heard some news about us. Just as if—Oh my God. If I didn't know better, I'd swear that Sister Dank had been acting as if she were under the impression that Imogene and I were getting married.

Tying the knot.

Getting hitched.

Entering into holy wedlock.

The second the thought entered my head, I went cold all over. I actually felt a little sick to my stomach. My God, could this be true? If Sister Dank was under the impression that Imogene and I were getting married, where could she have gotten such an idea?

Of course, the minute I asked myself the question, I could hear in my mind Brother Tallman saying, right after I'd complained that everybody in Pigeon Fork was going to think that I'd been in his office confessing something unmentionable, *"I'll take care of it, OK? It'll be fine."* Good Lord. Was this how Brother Tallman had taken care of it? He'd told his church secretary that I had not been in his office confessing. I'd been in there, asking him to marry me and Imogene? Was he nuts?

My mouth actually went dry at the thought. What was really scary was that, if I was right and Sister Dank thought that Imogene and I were getting married, she certainly did not seem like the type to keep this little news tidbit to herself. Oh no, it would be all over Pigeon Fork by daybreak.

Imogene would, no doubt, hear about it. And be expecting me to propose.

Oh my God.

How the hell was I going to get out of this one?

Don't get me wrong. There is absolutely nothing wrong with Imogene. All I had to do was think about her and I'd find myself smiling.

Sure, I suppose there are those who'd say that Imogene is not exactly beautiful, but I sure wouldn't be one of them. With shoulder-length wavy brown hair, a creamy complexion, and curves in all the right places, she is—in my opinion—downright gorgeous, in a big-boned, farm-fresh sort of way.

True, I might not have thought so the first time I saw her, but she wasn't having one of her best days. Her poor sister had just been murdered, and Pigeon Fork's twin deputies, Jeb and Fred Gunterman, were trying to keep her out of the crime scene. As I recall, Imogene kicked both of them in the shins.

Considering the fact that the Gunterman twins are real big guys, so much so that the two of them are known around town as the "Two-Ton Twins," right away I'd admired Imogene's courage. She'd even called Jeb and Fred "goons" right to their faces, a thing that had left me slack-jawed with amazement. What amazed me most was that nobody ever says anything to the twins' faces, mainly because their identical faces—with their beefy jaws, short pug noses, and tiny eyes—look downright scary.

Oh yeah. Imogene is a real gutsy woman. It is one of the things I love about her. Fact is, I don't doubt for an instant that I love everything about her. I don't even doubt that she'd make a real fine wife.

The thing is, though, I've already done the marriage thing. To put the very best possible face on the whole experience, I believe a root canal would've been a lot less painful. And, no doubt, considerably less expensive. I had married Claudzilla for richer or for poorer, and she'd made damn sure that the one I was going to end up with was *poorer.*

I only just paid off the last of the credit cards that Claudzilla was so kind as to leave me with.

So was I ready to get married for the second time? Not only no, but hell, no.

I parked my truck in the garage and headed toward the steps leading to my deck and front door. Rip, of course, was still carrying on something awful. From the racket he was making, you'd have thought I was wearing a mask and carrying a large bag to carry away loot.

Usually, at this point, I'm pretty irritated that Rip does not seem to recognize me as the guy who feeds him, for God's sake, and I'm yelling at him to shut up. Today, though, I stopped and watched his shenanigans for a moment before I began the climb up to my front deck.

"Attaboy, Rip," I said, "we don't want to get married again, now do we?"

The very idea appeared to send Rip into a fit. Of course, this was the sort of thing he did every single night when I got home—his own personal interpretation of Cujo after the rabies symptoms kicked in big time. Tonight, though, he did it up big. Snarling, and barking, and slobbering, and jumping up and down in a frenzy of motion. It seemed to me as if he was even more enraged than usual. In fact, a couple of times he barked with such force that he knocked himself off his own feet. Both times, though, he got up again with a look on his furry face that said, "I meant to do that."

"Good boy, Rip, good boy," I said, "that's what we think of getting married, isn't it? It knocks us for a loop. *That's* what we think of that idea." I was climbing the stairs by then, and Rip stopped in mid-bark to cock his head to one side and just look at me. I think it had taken him until then to realize that I was not yelling at him the way I usually do, but actually seemed to be praising him. He was giving me his what-the-hell-is-going-on look.

I was almost to the top of the deck by now, so Rip did what he always does. He dropped his Cujo impression and started doing a scene from *Lassie Come Home*. You would've thought that fool dog hadn't seen me in years, the way he carried on, wriggling all over and dancing back and forth and occasionally leaping in the air with joy. If I had not known that Rip goes through this same routine whether I've been gone for a day, or just five minutes down to the grocery store, I might've been more touched.

"Good boy, Rip, good boy," I said again. This is evidently something Rip can't hear enough of. He seemed to go wild, wriggling all over and leaping back and forth in hysterical frenzy.

When I was almost to the top step, Rip abruptly cut the hysterics and scooted over as far as he dared to the edge of the deck. There, as usual, he waited. For me to, yes, pick him up, squirming, and whining, and licking, and carry him down to the side yard.

As soon as I reached for him, Rip sprang into my arms. I guess I should've known that by this time, he was desperate. Unfortunately, the possibility of my impending nuptials had blown my mind so bad that Rip caught me unawares. His leap nearly knocked me over backwards, so that I stumbled halfway back downstairs before I regained my balance. I let out a yell, and then I said, "Rip, never, never, never jump on me. OK, boy? NEVER." I don't know why I was telling him this. The dog obviously did not speak my language. He kept right on squirming and trying to lick my face until I put him down on the grass.

When Rip was through decorating my side yard, I picked him up again and carried him back up to the deck. Rip this time gave up on licking my face and tried instead to lick my ears. I think he does this because my ears are easier to get to. Or maybe because he knows I hate it. "No, boy, no, boy, no, No, NO! NO! NO!"

"No" is, I think, the word I use most often with Rip, and yet, after seven years, it's a word he still can't seem to grasp. He kept right on aiming his wet, sloppy tongue in the direction of my ears until I got him up on the deck.

"I said NO, Rip," I told him. "NO. As in, No, I don't want to get married. No, I'm not getting married. NO, I have no intention of getting married. NO, NO, NO!"

I let Rip jump down onto the deck, and I headed for my front door. I didn't have to unlock the thing. Out here, pretty much in the middle of nowhere, I figure if a burglar has come all this way, and braved my hill, then he pretty much deserves whatever he can find inside worth stealing. I do wish he'd leave me a note as to what he considered worth taking, just for my information, but other than that, he was welcome to it.

Thinking about Imogene and wedlock had made my stomach start hurting pretty bad, so I decided that as soon as I went inside, I was going to do two things. First, I needed to take a large swig from the big bottle of Maalox that I keep in my refrigerator for just such an occasion. I've always thought that the advertising campaign for milk would've been a lot more apropos for an antacid. *Got Maalox?* Now there's a slogan I could identify with.

Second, I dialed long-distance to the Louisville Police Department to talk to my friend who shall remain nameless. I hadn't talked to Nameless in quite some time, so I wasn't sure if he was still on second shift. I did know, however, that whoever answered the phone would probably know when Nameless would be coming in.

Wouldn't you know it, Nameless himself answered the phone. I was kind of flattered that even after all this time, he instantly recognized my voice. "Hey, Haskell," he said. "Long time, no hear from, old buddy. What can I do for you?"

The nice thing about Nameless is that you never have to remind him that he owes you. He knows it, and he's way ahead of you. You don't even have to bother with the usual "How's the wife and kids?" because Nameless doesn't like small talk. He always cuts to the chase.

I filled him in with everything I knew about Bailey Prather, which wasn't a whole lot. And I told him about Sister Tallman's being Prather's spiritual advisor. And finally, I said that I'd really appreciate hearing anything about Prather that he could find out.

Nameless's answer was short and sweet. "Sure thing." He told me he'd call me back as soon as he found out anything, and then he hung up.

I thought it might even be the next day before I heard back from Nameless, but it was only about an hour later that the phone rang. "Wow," Nameless said as soon as I answered. "You sure can pick 'em."

"I can?" I'd been cooking myself a hot dog in the microwave and nuking me a bowl of Campbell's vegetable beef. I was pretty sure he wasn't referring to my choice of supper menu. "What do you mean?" Balancing the telephone receiver on my shoulder, I moved to my refrigerator and started looking for the mustard.

Rip had been watching me, particularly once I started cooking my Oscar Mayer, and he padded over to the refrigerator with me. Just in case I needed some canine help, I guess. Or—and this was a lot more likely—just in case I got clumsy and dropped something that needed eating.

"What I mean is," Nameless said, "Bailey Prather is one slimy little toad. A first-class asshole. A total degenerate. A—"

Nameless always did enjoy calling criminal-types ugly names, and I would've let him indulge himself to his heart's content except that I was kind of anxious to hear what he'd found out. I interrupted. "So what did Prather do to get to be a degenerate?"

"Robbed the Burleytown Credit Union, for one thing. Just took that place to the cleaners."

Burleytown is a sleepy Kentucky town even smaller than Pigeon Fork. I was a little surprised Burleytown even *had* a credit union. Let alone that Prather had robbed it.

"Can you imagine?" Nameless went on. "Prather went to work for the credit union as a teller, and one day he just walked into the safe and helped himself to every single penny that was there."

I didn't hesitate. I asked the question I'd been wondering about ever since Sister Dank had mentioned the robbery earlier. "How much did he get away with?"

Nameless snorted, a pretty ugly sound to hear while you're fixing yourself something to eat. "This'll kill you. According to my cuz, Prather stole two hundred and fifty thou and some change!"

Why wasn't I surprised? "Did they ever recover the money?" I was still looking for the mustard. I was sure I had some, but I'd searched all the shelves in the refrigerator and come up empty.

Nameless laughed. "They've never recovered so much as a thin dime. They would've known it, too, if any of the money had shown up anywhere, because the serial numbers of the bills had all been recorded at the credit union."

"Then what you're telling me is, Prather was going to have to launder the money in some way." I was looking in a sandwich bag filled with condiments from various fast-food stores. There was ketchup, salt, pepper, sweet and sour sauce, but no mustard. And how could I possibly eat a hot dog without mustard?

"Well, now, Haskell," Nameless said, "he only had to launder it if he was going to actually spend it. If he was going to use it to stuff a mattress, it would be fine the way it was."

Nameless always did have a weird sense of humor.

"Of course," he hurried on, "the way Prather tells it, there is no money. Not anymore. Seems our boy had this terrible fire at his house, right after the robbery at the credit union, and a long time before they finally arrested him. Everything inside burned to a crisp. According to Prather, the money was in the house. And, hey, I believe him, sure I do, every single word. I mean, why on earth would he lie about a thing like that?"

I lifted an ancient box of baking soda and looked behind it. "Why did it take so long to arrest him?"

Nameless snorted again, something he needed to stop doing over the phone. "Can you believe it, they couldn't get anybody to agree to testify against him. Seems this guy is something of a ladies' man."

I'd just located a small jar of mustard, wedged in the door of my refrigerator between a jar of olives that had been in there so long that they were more brown than green, and a jar of maraschino cherries that I'd bought two Christmases ago. What Nameless had just said, though, made me almost drop the phone and the mustard both.

A ladies' man? Was it possible that Sister Tallman had been taken in by this guy? Could he have been using her and the Pentecostal Church bank account to launder his money?

"Him being a ladies' man is what finally brought him down, though. It turned out that he was having an affair with several of the women at the credit union all at the same time. None of them wanted to rat on him at first. Then they found out about each other. After that they were stumbling all over themselves, racing to be the first one to throw him under the bus. According to my cousin, three different women testified at Prather's trial.

And every one of them looked angry enough to spit nails."

"Wow," I said. I was beginning to be in awe of this Bailey Prather guy.

"Wow is right," Nameless said. "This turkey's got a rap sheet a mile long. A few years back, he swindled some woman in her sixties, got her to sign over her house to him, and then he put her in a nursing home. He's borrowed money from countless women, and then sort of forgot to pay it back."

"He's a con artist," I said. Speaking of which, Rip had moved to stand right in front of the part of the kitchen counter that held the plate with my hot dog on it. His nose moved slowly in that direction, his big brown eyes watching me every inch of the way.

"Conning women," Nameless said. "From what my cousin said, this asshole should be behind bars for the rest of his life, if you only count half the crap he's pulled. And yet, they're letting him out day after tomorrow."

I'd been studying Rip, wondering when he was going to make his move on my hot dog, but now I almost dropped the mustard again. "What do you mean, he's getting out?"

"Sorry to tell you this, old buddy, but my cuz says that Bailey Prather has served his time. He was in for ten to twenty for robbery, and they gave him time off for good behavior." Nameless made another snorting noise that came through clear as anything over the phone. "Of course, you and I know they also gave him time off because the prison system is pretty much overloaded these days. And if they can let anybody out, they will."

I was still juggling the phone and the mustard. And trying to keep Rip's nose away from my hot dog. Not an easy job. "So Bailey Prather has been paroled? He's getting out of Eddyville?"

"He's just got one more day, and he's free as a bird," Nameless said. "He'll be out on parole day after tomorrow."

"Day after tomorrow? That sure doesn't leave me much time."

Nameless snorted yet again. "You got that right. If you want to have a little talk with the boy, you'd better do it tomorrow. Because after that, old Bailey is gonna have a brand-new address."

Not to mention, with a quarter of a million dollars in traveling money, Bailey Prather's new address could be in another country.

It looked to me as if I needed to talk to him fast.

§
§

The next morning I got up, showered, shaved, got dressed, and made the round trip to the side yard carrying Rip, who squirmed and tried to lick my ears every step of the way. Dodging Rip's tongue, I deposited him back on my deck, filled his bowls with water and Gravy Train, and started to head out the door, with my nose pretty much pointed in the direction of Eddyville.

Unfortunately, I didn't keep my nose pointed in that direction. It occurred to me that before I left, I really ought to phone my office and let Melba know where I was going to be. And to pick up any messages, just in case Hell had frozen over yesterday, and Melba had not only answered my phone but she'd actually recorded who had called and how to reach them.

Hey, I knew it was a long shot, but stranger things have happened.

Melba answered on the fourth ring with her usual professionalism. "What?" She sounded irritated at having her morning disturbed.

"Melba, I believe I've mentioned how I'd like my phone to be answered." Actually, I believe I'd mentioned it, oh, about a hundred times. *Haskell Blevins Investigations.* That's all I've asked her to say. At one time, I'd also wanted her to say *Good morning* or *Good afternoon* before she said the name, but I'd soon realized that asking Melba to determine whether it was morning or afternoon in addition to answering the phone was asking a tad too much.

"Oh, it's you," Melba said. Her entire tone changed. Oddly enough, she actually sounded glad to hear from me. "Well, hi Haskell! How in the world are ya doing?"

This might've been the first time in our entire professional relationship that Melba had ever asked me how I was doing. Up until now I'd pretty much figured that I could be lying at her feet, with blood spurting from open wounds, and Melba would simply step over me on her way to her desk.

She certainly would not pause—not even for a split second—to ask how I was doing.

I might've wondered why Melba was suddenly interested in my well-being now. I might have also tried to figure out what had brought on this little mood change. I decided, though, that it would be sort of like trying to figure out why the last Kentucky Lottery scratch-off you'd bought had finally paid off. When you came right down to it, who cared, as long as you were winning?

While Melba was still in a halfway decent mood, I thought I'd make sure she'd heard what I'd just said. "Melba, didn't I tell you how I'd like my phone to be answered?"

"Oh yeah, you've told me, all right," Melba said, "but it's too late now, Haskell. I've already answered the phone." She made it sound as if she were telling me something I didn't already know.

"You do remember what I wanted you to say, though?" I wasn't trying to pick a fight, I was just checking, that's all. Just making sure that my communication skills were not lacking.

"Yeah, Haskell, I remember, OK?" Melba said. Her tone was on a downhill slide. "Haskell Blevins Investigations. Are you happy now?"

"Overjoyed," I said.

Melba made a smacking noise that I immediately recognized as the noise she makes with gum. "You needn't take that tone with me, Haskell. You know damn well that it's pretty pointless to go on and on about how I'm supposed to answer the damn phone when I've already done it. So, unless you want to call back,

I don't see any reason to keep on yammering about it, do you?"

What could I say? She had a point. Not to mention, since I was about to go out of town, I really hated to get on Melba's bad side. Melba, when she's in a good mood, does a pretty bad job. When she's in a bad mood, though, she does a job so bad, it's scary. She's as likely to hang up on clients as she is to curse them out. Once, when I'd jumped on her about hiding my filing, she'd told everybody who phoned that I'd gone out of business. Later, she told me she'd only said that because she'd been too depressed to write down any messages.

I, of course, had been considerably depressed to hear it.

In the interest of avoiding depression altogether, I decided not to yammer. I also decided to change the subject. "So, Melba, do I have any messages?"

"Just one," she said. "From Imogene." Oddly enough, Melba sort of sang Imogene's name. *Em-oh-ge-e-e-en.* "She said she can meet you for dinner tonight, if you're free. She's gonna be getting back in town earlier than she thought."

Any other time, I'd have been grinning up a storm, just knowing I was going to see Imogene tonight. That, however, was before I started worrying about what rumors Imogene might be hearing once she got back in town. Now hearing that she was returning early made my stomach hurt. Bad.

"Imogene said she tried to call you at home," Melba hurried on, "but you weren't there."

I wondered if she'd called when I'd been at the Pentecostal Church.

"And then," Melba went on, "she had to go to another seminar or class or something—I can't remember exactly what she said, can you believe it—?"

Hey, I could believe it.

"—but Imogene did say that she'd check back in with you sometime today."

My mouth had actually gone dry. I had to swallow once before I spoke, so Melba wouldn't be able to tell how rattled I was. "Well, now, that's gonna be a problem," I said. "I'm going to be out of town the entire day, so Imogene won't be able to—"

"I'll be glad to give Imogene a message for you," Melba said, interrupting me. "*Glad* to!" Melba actually sounded tickled pink, as if maybe she was looking forward to talking to Imogene.

The thought of Melba the Mouth having any conversation whatsoever with Imogene made my mouth go even more dry. I believe tumbleweeds were now blowing past my tonsils.

"So, Haskell, hon, you want me to tell your lady that you'll meet her somewhere, or were you planning an intimate little dinner for just you two, you sly dog?"

Sly dog? Since when had I become a sly dog? Not to mention, since when had Melba started calling me "hon"? "Excuse me?" I said.

"Oh, now, Haskell, you're not going to try and tell me that you're not planning anything special for when Imogene gets back, because I know you're planning something." Melba actually giggled at this point. Really. A grown woman, and she giggled. "Personally, I just want to be the first to tell you how happy I am for you two. I just think, well, I just think it's great. It's wonderful, wonderful, wonderful news!"

Oh God. The last time I'd heard Melba this excited, the Coke machine at Elmo's had broken down and it was dispensing Cokes for free and giving you change.

I tried to keep calm, but to tell the truth, my heart had speeded up some. "Uh, Melba," I said, "I don't suppose, when you say that I'm planning something, that you're talking about my planning on taking Imogene to the movies or something like that?"

Melba hooted at that one. "Oh, Haskell, you are the cutest! You *are!*"

I cleared my throat. "Melba, what did you hear about me and Imogene? Exactly?"

"Oh, you silly goose, it's all over town! About how you and your lovely lady are going to walk down the aisle! I'm not sure who told Elmo, but Elmo told me."

"Oh my God."

I didn't realize I'd said this aloud until Melba said, "Oh, now, Haskell, don't get upset. If you want this to be a big secret, well then, so be it! You can surprise Imogene if you want to, you cutie! I won't tell Imogene a thing, OK? Not a thing!"

I could have pointed out to Melba that, if what she'd just told me was true, then she was not the only person in town who would have to keep quiet. I didn't think I was being overly pessimistic to think that anything continuing to be a big secret when all of Pigeon Fork was talking about it was pretty remote. I was suddenly feeling far too rattled, though, to discuss any of this with Melba.

"But, Haskell, hon," Melba was going on, "even if you do want it to be a big secret, I do wanna say just one thing. I—well, I just think it's wonderful! I really do! It's wonderful, wonderful, wonderful!"

Hadn't she just said that? What was it with the women in this town? The divorce rate in Pigeon Fork is pretty much what it is everywhere else in America—one out of two marriages goes belly up—and yet every woman in town still gets ecstatic when they think somebody's getting married. Come to think of it, in Pigeon Fork, the divorce rate is probably a little higher than everywhere else, being as how kids around these parts are less likely to go to college and more likely to get hitched right out of high school. Which pretty much guarantees that they'll be getting unhitched before they turn thirty.

Not to mention, it's the nineties, for God's sakes. Aren't women supposed to be wanting to get fulfilled these days, have a career first, and postpone marriage and family? Apparently, the womenfolk in Pigeon Fork hadn't heard about any of this stuff. They'd heard about my impending nuptials, but they hadn't heard about getting fulfilled, or working outside the house, or putting off having kids. Oh no, they are too busy being delirious whenever they find out that somebody is getting married off.

I've never understood exactly why it is that these women get so all-fired happy when they hear of wedding plans. If I were even more cynical than I already am, I'd say that it was just that misery loves company. Or maybe that all the women around these parts have got attorneys somewhere in their families, and they know full well that fifty percent of the time, a new marriage eventually means job security for this particular relative of theirs. Or could it be that all these women just take some kind of perverse pleasure out of knowing that another man has bitten the dust? As far as Melba was concerned, I pretty much leaned toward that last scenario.

She was still chuckling over the phone. "Oh yeah, Haskell, you and Imogene make the cutest, cutest, cutest couple!"

Three "cutests." In addition to the three "wonderfuls?" This was getting ugly. I told Melba to tell Imogene that I'd call her after I returned from Eddyville, and then I hung up. After which I did what I'd been wanting to do ever since I'd first heard the rumor floating around about Imogene and me.

I got out of town.

It took me not quite three hours to get to Eddyville. Most of the drive was on Western Kentucky Parkway. It's a pretty dull drive, just winding blacktop going past farmland on both sides of the highway, with only an occasional barn or a house to break the monotony. After a while it's just fields and trees on one side of the highway, and then for variety, trees and fields on the other side. It's the kind of road that makes you understand how people can fall asleep at the wheel.

There were only two things even close to interesting that I passed on the way. The first was a small farm consisting of a dilapidated frame farmhouse badly in need of paint, a ramshackle barn, a silo, and assorted sheds. None of that was particularly unusual, except that right in front of the house was a large

sign, facing the highway. It simply said For
Sale and gave a local phone number. The sign
itself was sadly not all that unusual a thing to
see these days. A whole lot of farmers in this
neck of the woods seem to be finding out that
you just can't make a living running the family
farm anymore. What made me notice this particular farm, though, was that this one looked
as if whoever had been farming his land had
just given up real sudden-like. There was still a
field of corn standing right by the edge of the
highway. Unharvested. In the middle of February, for God's sake. In fact, it looked as if the
farmer had up and decided one day that it
wasn't even worth harvesting his last crop. Or
maybe the guy had died, and his heirs had decided it was too much trouble to harvest the
corn. Whatever the story, it wasn't every day
you see a cornfield in the middle of the winter
with the corn still in it. Some of the gray-
brown stalks were broken and lying every
which way, but a whole lot of it was still
standing.

It made you feel kind of sad, looking at it. It
was like looking at corn ghosts haunting a
field.

The second thing I saw that was halfway interesting was another old farm. This one had a
big pond with several duck decoys floating in
it. What made me kind of perk up a little as I
went zooming by, though, was not the duck

decoys. It was what was standing on the wide expanse of lawn between the pond and the farmhouse—two life-size black-and-white cow statues. Really. Two large stone holstein cows. It looked as if the farmer had put out cow decoys, too. In order—of course—to attract a few live cows, along with a few live ducks. In winter. That farmer must've been a real optimist.

OK, at this point, I knew I was beginning to think very strange thoughts. Cow decoys not being a topic I usually pondered. This, however, is the sort of thing that happens when you're traveling the monotony of Western Kentucky Parkway, trying not to fall asleep. And trying not to think about whether or not your girlfriend is going to be expecting you to get down on bended knee when you get back home.

By the time I got to US 62 and the Eddyville exit, I had my window rolled down on the driver's side and my radio blaring just to keep myself awake. It didn't help that just about the only music you can get around these parts is country. It's not the kind of country that sounds a lot like what they used to call pop, either. It's the kind of country in which the singer generally sings with what sounds like a nasal condition and a bad case of hiccups.

Dwight Yokum was hiccuping through yet another she-done-me-wrong song as I turned onto the road leading to Eddyville Prison. Actually, most folks in Kentucky just call the place Eddyville, but residents of the town of Eddyville get a tad put out if you do that. Apparently, they don't like people thinking that when they say "I live in Eddyville," they're talking about the prison. I reckon they're just sensitive that way.

Eddyville Prison's real name is the Kentucky State Penitentiary, which I believe anybody would agree sounds a lot more impressive. The Kentucky State Penitentiary is the only maximum-security prison in Kentucky, but it sure doesn't look like the kind of prison you see on television and at the movies. You know—stark and grim like Attica or Alcatraz. What Eddyville looks like is a large, stone, medieval castle with turrets on all four corners. In fact, folks in Kentucky actually call the thing "the Castle on the Cumberland." Every time I've heard somebody say this, though, it's always given me pause. For one thing, I'm pretty sure the royalty housed in the Castle would not see the humor in this little phrase.

For another, I can't quite understand why the thing is called the Castle on the Cumberland. I understand the castle part, of course. It's the rest of it I don't get. Mainly because it's not the Cumberland that the prison overlooks, it's Lake Barkley. I realize that the folks inside the prison don't get out much, so maybe they're under the impression that it really is the Cumberland out there. You'd think, though, that if they couldn't check it out personally they'd just ask somebody. *Hey, what's the name of that big body of water right next to the prison?* Or maybe they could just look at a map, for God's sake.

The huge structure is over a century old, but it sure doesn't look any the worse for wear. The stone walls look like they might still be standing a long time after, oh, say, the Pyramids have fallen into disrepair.

I've always thought it was kind of ironic that Eddyville Prison is situated on Lake Barkley, one of Kentucky's more scenic vacation spots. Lake Barkley is real popular with the tourists, too. I've often wondered if any of the convicts inside could actually see from the windows in their cells all the vacationers happily boating and swimming out on the lake.

In some cases, I'd say that might amount to cruel and unusual punishment.

In other cases, though, considering what crimes had been committed to get their perpetrators accommodations behind bars, I believe it would only be fair if their cells came equipped with binoculars. And maybe have a few travel brochures lying around, describing Lake Barkley and the adjacent Land between the Lakes in colorful detail.

I parked my truck and headed inside. Nameless's cousin had evidently worked a minor miracle on my behalf. Generally, when you visit a prisoner, you have to stand in line and be searched, and fill out papers and do an awful lot of things that take up an ungodly amount of time. Thanks to the magic of Nameless's cousin, everything had already been arranged.

After going through several doors and checking in with several guards, I was shown into a room with nothing in it but a scarred wooden table and two metal chairs. I sat down in one of the chairs, and I waited. I expected to wait for quite a while, but in no time at all, the door opened and a prison guard walked in. Stepping to one side, the guard stood rather stiffly to the left of the door as a small man, about five feet eight, sauntered in.

I stared at him.

This couldn't be Bailey Prather. The ladies' man? Burleytown, Kentucky's answer to Casanova? Had there been some kind of mistake? This guy had thinning brown hair, rounded shoulders, John Lennon wire-rimmed glasses, and he couldn't have weighed more than a hundred fifty pounds. He wasn't ugly or anything—probably very few animals and children ran at the sight of him—but he sure wasn't what you'd call handsome either.

I tried not to stare, but I couldn't help it. According to Nameless, *this* was the guy who'd slept with three different women at the credit union in Burleytown?

Hell, Bailey Prather was an inspiration to us all.

He stared back at me for a long moment, studying my face, obviously trying to place me. Finally, he broke into an easy grin. "OK, I give up. I don't know who the hell you are," he said. Prather had a softer Southern accent than you get from living in Kentucky. I guessed him to be from Alabama or Georgia. "But whoever you are," he went on, "it's right kind of you to drop by and pay me a visit on my last day in this place."

I cleared my throat. "I'm Haskell Blevins." I would've shaken Prather's hand, but there are rules about that here at Eddyville. You don't touch the prisoners. Ever. Even if they're heading out the door the very next day, you keep your hands to yourself.

Prather sure didn't seem to expect it. He just stood there looking at me, his blue eyes behind the wire-rims curious and amused. "Haskell Blevins, huh? Hmm. Well, your name sounds somewhat familiar, but I can't place it." He grinned again and ran his hand through his thinning hair. "To tell you the truth, though, it don't much matter who you are. I'd much prefer being in here, talking to a complete stranger, than sitting in my damn jail cell, waiting for the clock to tick off the minutes."

It was nice to know that talking to me could beat out spending time behind bars. I mean, a thing like that could really boost the old ego.

I reckon Bailey must've known what I was thinking, because he was now grinning up a storm. "It's right nice of whoever-you-are to break up this day for me. Because, you know, even though folks might think otherwise—prison being such a nice place to live and all—your last day inside, I don't know, it always just *drags* something awful. Can't imagine why." He outright laughed now, as if what he'd just said was a real hoot.

"It *always* drags?" I said. "Then you've been paroled before?"

Prather shrugged and grinned. He did not look the least bit embarrassed to tell me, "Let's just say that I have been a guest of the state several times over the course of my life." He grinned and added, "I suppose I just can't resist having a free roof over my head and three squares a day. I mean, it's such a bargain!" Moving across the room, he turned a chair around backwards, swung his leg over it, and sat down, leaning his arms on the back of the chair. I wasn't sure if Prather's body language was supposed to tell me something, but the chair had metal slats on it, so it seemed to me that, even as Bailey and I were talking, there were still bars between us. "So, Mr. Blevins, as much as I appreciate your thinking of me and all, I am a little curious as to what brings you to this neck of the woods," Prather said. "Surely you've got better things to do than drop by a prison."

"Call me Haskell," I said. "I'm a private detective."

Prather didn't so much laugh this time as chuckle a little.

"I'm investigating—" That was all I got out before Prather held up his hand as if signaling me to stop.

"OK, Haskell," Prather said, "you might as well stop right there. You're wasting your time."

I blinked at that one. "How do you figure?"

Prather laughed again. The man must've had a remarkable sense of humor, because everything seemed to crack him up. "Well, you're here about the money, aren't you? You know, the quarter of a million I took from that credit union?"

I just looked at him blankly, and what do you know, he hurried on.

"Now don't you be playing games with me, Haskell. I'm talking about the *money*. You know, the reason I'm here. Don't go playing dumb with me, I know everybody at the Burleytown Credit Union thinks I've still got all that money."

"They do." I said it without any inflection so

Prather wouldn't be able to tell if I was agreeing with him or not.

"Well," he hurried on, "I hate to break it to you—"

Prather didn't look as if he hated it. He looked as if he were enjoying himself.

"—but the money burned up. All of it. If you'll read the newspaper dated about a week after the robbery, you'll find out that my house burned to the ground. And it's like I told the police, the money was there. In the house, see? So when the house burned, it burned, too."

I just stared at him. For a man who'd just spent a few years in prison for stealing a lot of money that he never got to spend, he looked downright cheerful. Of course, he was getting out of prison tomorrow. That could possibly lift a man's spirits some.

Prather was leaning forward now, propping his arms on the back of the chair. "Do you get what I'm telling ya? The money is nothing but ashes now." Prather smiled and ran his hand through his thinning hair again. "And take my word for it, Haskell, you'll make an *ash* of yourself if you keep looking for it."

He grinned at his little joke.

He wanted me to take his word, and he was in *prison* for God's sake. I could be jumping to conclusions here, but it seemed to me that it was highly unlikely that there were a whole lot of real trustworthy folks occupying prison cells. Call me cynical.

"I don't know anything about any credit union," I lied. "What I'm here about is something else entirely. I've been helping out the reverend at the Pentecostal Church of the Holy Scriptures. I reckon you've heard of it?"

The minute I said the name of the church, something flashed in Prather's blue eyes. It was gone in an instant, though. By the time I had gotten the whole name of the church out, he was looking as if he'd never heard of the place. "Pentecostal Church? Hmmm," Prather said, tapping his chin. "Doesn't ring a bell."

Yeah, right. "Really?" I said. "That's kinda strange. Sister Tallman, the wife of the minister of the Pentecostal Church of the Holy Scriptures—well, I believe she's been visiting you quite often."

Prather just looked at me for a long moment without saying a word. I couldn't be sure, of course, but it looked to me as if he was trying to decide whether to answer or not.

I stared right back at him. He could not be called—in any way, shape, or form—handsome. So how in the world did he have such a way with women? Riddle me that, Batman.

Prather snapped his fingers as if he'd suddenly remembered something. "Oh, *Sister Tallman* . . ." He tried to sound as if it had not occurred to him before that moment that

Sister Tallman's church was the Pentecostal
Church of the Holy Scriptures. "Sure. I remember now. Sister Tallman is a real fine
lady." Prather seemed to have a way of saying
things that made you wonder whether he was
serious or not. "Oh yeah," he went on, "Kay
Fay's been a real help to me. In my rehabilita-
tion."

"Kay Fay?" I repeated. They were on a first-
name basis?

Prather's eyes did that flashing thing again.
"Well, what I meant to say was Sister Tallman,
of course."

I gave him a quick smile. "Of course," I said.

Prather's grin grew wider. "Yeah, Sister Tallman is my spiritual advisor. She's been trying
to help me turn from my path of wickedness,
and start—you know—walking the straight
and narrow."

I just looked at him. Prather did seem to be
enjoying himself. His eyes were all but dancing behind his wire-rims. If I didn't know
better, I'd think he knew a secret I didn't
know—and that the secret was so terrific, it
actually pained him a little not to get to tell
me all about it and gloat a little.

"Well," I said, "that's what I wanted to ask
you about. There's been a little problem at the
church, and I wonder if Sister Tallman ever
mentioned anything about it to you." I was
fudging big time here. I really didn't expect to

get anything close to a straight answer from Prather. Mainly, what I wanted to do was see his reaction. Was it really possible he was using Sister Tallman and the church bank account to launder his stolen funds?

Prather pushed his chair back from the table and, putting his hands behind his head, stretched out some. I think if the guard had not been there eyeing him, he would've propped his feet on the table.

I just looked at him. It didn't seem possible for the man to look any more relaxed. "So," Prather drawled, "what kind of problem is the church having?"

I was the one who shrugged this time. "I'm really not at liberty to say."

At liberty is probably not a phrase you want to use when talking to a person who's incarcerated. Prather, however, didn't seem to notice. He just said, "Sister Tallman never mentioned any problems." He actually sounded genuinely puzzled. I had to hand it to him. Bailey Prather was either totally in the dark on this one, or he ought to be up for an Academy Award nomination this year for Best Actor Serving Jail Time. I scooted my chair away from the table, getting ready to get out of there. "Well, I guess that's all I—"

Prather interrupted me. He may have just been trying to make my visit last a little longer, but he stopped stretching and sat up rather abruptly, looking straight at me. "You're not going to leave before you ask me, are you?" He shook his head. "That would be a first."

He'd lost me. "Excuse me?"

Prather was grinning again. "I always get the same question. You are going to ask me, aren't you?"

I still just looked at him. "What do you mean?"

Prather's grin just kept getting wider. "What you've been wondering about ever since I first walked in here. You know, how I have such a way with the ladies? What my big secret is. How in the hell I've gotten to be such a babe magnet."

What a gentlemanly way to put that.

I would've loved to have told him that I could not care less, but the truth was, of course, I was downright curious. How the hell did he do it? I couldn't believe he was bringing up the subject for me. "Yeah, well, now that you mention it, I reckon I do."

Prather's grin could've wrapped around his face a couple times. "I bet you think I'm a real stud or something. Or that I'm hung like a mule."

Once again, a real gentlemanly thing to say. It was my guess that Prather did not talk like this around his lady friends.

"The thought never crossed my mind," I lied.

Prather leaned toward me and lowered his voice. "You'd be surprised what the real secret to getting women is."

His grin was beginning to irritate me. I restrained myself from leaning toward him and tried not to look too eager. "Oh yeah?" I said. "So what is it?"

Prather actually laughed, obviously pleased that he'd gotten me to outright ask him. "Well, Haskell, my man," he drawled, "I reckon I owe you if you've come all this way to pay me a visit on my last day here. So I tell you what I'm going to do."

"What?" I said warily.

"I'll look you up after I get outa here," Prather went on, "and I'll tell you my secret then. You live in Pigeon Fork, don't you?"

I nodded.

"Then we got us an appointment," Prather said, grinning to beat the band again. He got to his feet, glancing over at the guard. "Guess I'm ready to go back now." He turned toward the door, took a step toward it, and then turned back toward me.

"Hey, wait a minute," he said. *"Haskell Blevins?* That's your name? Why, you shouldn't be wanting tips on attracting the ladies, Haskell. Ain't you the one who's getting ready to pop the question?"

It was all I could do to keep my mouth from dropping open. "Where did you hear that?"

Prather winked at me. "I got my sources," he said. "Just like you private dicks do."

He headed out the door, still grinning big time, with the guard plodding along at Prather's heels like a faithful dog.

I, on the other hand, didn't move for quite some time. I just sat there like a bump on a pickle, watching Prather and the guard go and trying real hard not to look as if my mind had just been totally blown.

9
§

I left Eddyville about two o'clock in the afternoon, and I didn't get home until around six-thirty. Yep, it took me an entire hour and a half longer than it had taken me before. I reckon I might as well admit it. I dawdled. I took a little detour over to Madisonville to get me a Big Mac, and then a while later, I stopped off in Leitchfield for a milk shake at the Burger King. The rest of the time I drove as slowly as I could without folks coming up behind me and honking.

My mind, believe me, was going considerably faster than my truck. My mind, in fact, could probably have won the Indianapolis 500. I couldn't believe Bailey Prather, of all people, had heard the rumors about me and Imogene. The news then had traveled all the way to *Eddyville?* I was well aware, of course, that the grapevine around these parts was quite a bit more efficient than the *Pigeon Fork Gazette*, but I'd had no idea that the vine stretched clear across the state and into a prison.

Obviously, Prather had talked to somebody in Pigeon Fork either late last night or early this morning. That wouldn't have been difficult to do, though. As a convict about to be paroled, Prather would've had no trouble receiving or making phone calls.

The question was, Whom had he talked to? Sister Tallman, of course, was the obvious choice. And yet, I wondered. Could it have been someone else? The possibilities were necessarily limited to just those folks who might've actually had that particular piece of information to pass along. Knowing what I now knew about the efficiency of the grapevine around these parts, though, I'd say that the entire population of Pigeon Fork and surrounding counties could've heard the wonderful, wonderful, wonderful news about me and Imogene, and passed it on to Prather behind bars.

I had to face facts. If the rumor had been heard in Eddyville, behind prison walls, for God's sake, there was very little chance that Imogene could avoid hearing it in Pigeon Fork. Hell, she might've heard it already.

Just the thought made my throat tighten up.

It didn't take a detective to deduce the logical conclusion to this little scenario. The obvious answer was that there wasn't any way I could get out of it. I was going to have to ask Imogene to marry me. This particular thought, as I zipped along Western Kentucky Parkway, made my stomach hurt.

Let me see. My throat felt like a vise was tightening around it. My stomach felt as if I'd swallowed a few hundred hot coals. And my hands were clammy. My God, if I didn't stop thinking about getting married, I'd be lucky if I didn't need to call an ambulance as soon as I got home.

And yet, I couldn't seem to think of anything else. I was going to have to pop the question. Because I wouldn't hurt Imogene for the world. I really was crazy about that woman. She was sweet, and kind, and understanding.

She was so understanding, in fact, that I couldn't help but wonder if I could simply explain to Imogene that even though Pigeon Fork was ready for me to get married, I was not. I ran that possibility over in my mind as I passed a station wagon carrying a family of four: Mom and Dad in the front, a little boy about nine and a little girl about six in the back.

Station wagons are not something you see much anymore. Perfect little nuclear families like this one are not something you see much anymore, either. I glanced over at Mr. and Mrs. Nuclear, feeling almost envious—they looked so content and the children in the back looked so cute—it was like looking at a Norman Rockwell painting of the ideal American family.

Hey, maybe I'd been looking at this all wrong. Maybe it would be a wonderful thing, after all, me and Imogene getting married, starting a family of our own. I was trying to visualize how this would be when the little towheaded boy in the back of the station wagon noticed me looking over at him. He glanced toward the front of the car, giving his parents a hard stare.

And then he gave me the finger.

What an adorable little tyke. I was pretty sure that Norman Rockwell would not have included that little gesture in his painting. So much for the ideal American family.

Now that I thought about it, there was every chance—let's face it—that I wasn't ready to be anybody's dad yet. I had enough trouble just taking care of myself.

As much to prove just how mature I was as anything else, I stuck my tongue out at the kid in the station wagon. He responded by giving me the finger with his other hand. Apparently, the boy was ambidextrous. What a talented child.

His dad glanced over at me now, giving me a piercing look. I'd just finished sticking out my tongue, so I was pretty sure Dad hadn't seen any of it. It seemed like a good idea, though, to turn my attention back to the road before Dad showed me just how nuclear the parent of a nuclear family could get. I eased up on the accelerator so that the station wagon pulled away from me.

I didn't even glance at the ambidextrous kid as the station wagon went by me. I did, however, notice the bumper stickers on the back of the station wagon. One said MY SON IS ON THE HONOR ROLL AT SOUTH CHRISTIAN ELEMENTARY. Evidently, that kid had learned a few things that were not part of the curriculum. Another bumper sticker said THE FAMILY THAT PRAYS TOGETHER STAYS TOGETHER. I could be wrong, but if the kid was giving strangers the finger in elementary school, then by the time their ambidextrous son got to be a teenager, Mom and Dad might be praying that he didn't stay around them.

It kind of made you wonder if you ever wanted to have yourself a family at all. Of course, just asking Imogene to marry me didn't mean we'd start a family right away. Hell, it didn't even mean that we'd get married right away, did it? Maybe Imogene and I could have a real long engagement. Like, oh, say, ten to twenty years.

I realized, as soon as that last thought crossed my mind, that I was making our impending engagement sound an awful lot like a prison sentence. In my defense, I would like to point out that I was on my way home from *Eddyville*, for God's sake. If visiting a prison didn't put you in an incarcerated frame of mind, I don't know what would.

Speaking of incarcerated, old Rip had to be pretty eager right about now to be paroled to the side yard. The exit off the interstate that led to my house loomed up ahead, and I accelerated a little. Five minutes later, I was putting my truck in low gear and starting up my driveway. Halfway up, I started hearing Rip at the top of my hill. Carrying on the way that dumb dog always does whenever I come home.

You have to admire old Rip, though, to give such a convincing performance day after day after day. Rip had talent all right. Once again he was doing his personal impression of Cujo at the end of the movie after the rabies had kicked in big time. Rip was even slobbering a little as he danced back and forth up there on my deck.

My garage is not attached to my A-frame, and when I pulled up in front of my house, I noticed right away that the garage door was open. Apparently, I'd left my door open when I'd left this morning. This is not hard to do. I have an automatic garage door opener, with two remote controls. One remote I keep inside on an end table in my living room, as a sort of backup system. I use this one in case I've forgotten to close the garage door and I'm already inside the house. The other remote I keep attached to the driver's side visor in my truck. Although I almost always hit the remote control to close the garage door as I'm heading down my driveway, sometimes the thing just doesn't work. I'm not sure why. Maybe I'm traveling too fast or maybe I'm out of range—whatever the reason, my garage door ends up staying wide open all day long.

Since the door was already open, I started to pull my truck in. And then I thought better of it, and stopped and parked in front of the house instead. There was no use putting my truck in the garage if I intended to go back out, and depending on what Imogene wanted to do, I might be heading over to her house right soon.

I started to hit the automatic opener in order to close the door, but then I decided to take pity on poor Rip. Rip has always been a little afraid of the garage door. In fact, when he's out in the yard, I've noticed that he gives the front of the garage a wide berth, eyeing the door suspiciously every time he goes by it. I believe old Rip has decided that—since the garage door seems to move on its own sometimes—the door must be alive. A couple of times when I've closed the garage door using the remote, that dumb dog has actually barked and growled at the door. Even now, in the middle of his hysterics, Rip was giving the garage door occasional quick, nervous glances. As if making sure that, yes, the garage door was still over there. It hadn't moved toward him yet.

It's things like this that make a dog owner proud.

That and Rip carrying on like a rabid Saint Bernard.

He was doing his entire routine now—snarling, and slobbering, and barking, and quivering. Occasionally—for variety, no doubt—he would leap high into the air, apparently driven into a frenzy of fury by the approach of someone he knew.

Having to go through this with my own dog every single day of my life is one of the reasons I've been glad to live alone. I may get a little lonely sometimes, but at least there is no one else to witness the remarkable way in which my own dog does not seem to recognize me every single time I come home.

If anybody else were here—like, oh, say, Imogene, for instance—it could be a tad embarrassing.

Rip was building to a crescendo of canine fury as I got out of my truck and started toward the house. "OK, Rip, that's enough, you can stop now," I said. "I'm impressed."

Rip didn't even pause. He danced toward the edge of the stairs, glanced nervously at the garage, and then danced back, snarling and growling.

"Rip, it's me. OK? IT'S ME!"

It must be difficult to be a dog. You'd be pretty much sentenced to live out your life in a place where you didn't speak the language. Rip obviously did not speak mine. Once again, he didn't even pause. He just kept right on growling and dancing.

"No, Rip!" I said. "No, no, NO! It's me, OK? NO!"

This time Rip stopped mid-growl, cocked his head to one side, and stared at me as if trying to place me. I would've liked to think that my telling him *no* actually had sunk into his little pea brain, but the truth was, I was almost to the top of the steps by this time. This is where Rip always cuts his Cujo routine and replaces it with a touching moment from *Lassie Come Home*.

In a split second, as I picked him up, he became one big wriggly, wagging bundle of canine joy. While he licked my face and I tried to keep his tongue out of my ear, I hauled his lard butt out to the side yard.

When Rip was done, I carried him back upstairs. When we passed the garage door, he whined a little, so naturally—feeding Rip's neurosis, no doubt—I quickened my pace. He seemed downright happy to follow me inside, where the garage door couldn't get him.

Once inside I knew I couldn't put things off any longer. I headed into my kitchen with Rip at my heels, picked up the phone, and dialed.

Hearing Imogene's sweet voice on the other end sure made me feel a little better.

"Imogene! You're back!" I said. It was not an effort to sound downright delighted.

"Oh, yes, I'm back, all right," Imogene said. Oddly enough, she didn't sound quite as delighted as I did. In fact, there seemed to be something in her tone that wasn't usually there. A kind of tenseness. It could've been because she was tired from traveling and all, but it also could be something else. I wondered uneasily if she'd already heard the rumors.

Surely she didn't expect me to propose over the phone.

"Boy, have I missed you," I said. I wasn't lying. She'd only been gone three days, but it really did seem like years. "I'm really looking forward to seeing you, Imogene. So, you want to come over here and I'll broil us up some steaks?"

There was silence over the phone. "Well, Haskell," Imogene finally said. "I don't know, I think maybe—"

I interrupted her. If she'd already heard the rumors, maybe she was expecting me to do it up big. "Or would you like me to take you out to a fancy restaurant."

There was not the slightest bit of hesitation this time. "Oh no!" Imogene said. "I don't want you to do that." She coughed, and then added,

"What I mean is, well, I guess I'm just not in the mood to eat out."

"Are you sure?" I said. "Because I'd be real happy to walk into one of them high-class restaurants with a pretty woman like you on my arm."

Oh yes, I am a silver-tongued devil.

Imogene sounded a little flustered. "I—I don't think so, Haskell. I'm real tired. After driving here all the way from Louisville, I really don't feel like getting back in the car and going for another long drive."

It was true. Getting to a real fine restaurant from Pigeon Fork would take some driving. The fanciest restaurant we've got within an hour's driving distance is Gentry's Family Restaurant and U-Pick-em Farm, which is up I-65 a piece going toward Louisville. I'm not sure it would qualify as all that fancy, either, being as how Gentry's has plastic place mats, and paper napkins, and, this time of year, not a fresh flower but a plastic one sticking out of a vase in the middle of every table. For that touch of authenticity, Mama Gentry always fills each vase with water, too. Unfortunately, this little detail does not make her plastic posies look any more real. It just looks as if Mama fully expects her plastic flowers to grow.

To get to a genuine fancy restaurant would mean driving all the way back into Louisville.

Too late, I realized I could've just met Imogene in Louisville tonight and we could've gone out to dinner there. I could've proposed to her before she'd even had a chance to hear the rumors back here. Damn. I could've kicked myself.

"Why don't you just come over to my place, Haskell," Imogene was saying, "and I'll cook us up something?"

She was too tired to sit in a car and go to a restaurant, and yet she would go to the trouble of fixing me dinner? Was this a wonderful woman or what? And yet, I couldn't possibly let Imogene fix dinner if I was going to ask her to marry me. I mean, my God, why didn't I just let her do a few loads of laundry, mop some floors, vacuum a little, dust, and then I'd pop the question? "Nope," I said, "I don't want you to have to make dinner after your long drive home, Imogene. I want you to be able to relax. So why don't you come over here, and I'll do the cooking?"

I was kind of surprised, but Imogene hesitated even then. "I don't know, Haskell, I'm real tired." Her voice did sound weary. "Maybe we ought to put off getting together tonight—"

Any other time I might've started getting my feelings hurt, on account of it beginning to sound as if Imogene might not be as anxious to see me as I was to see her. This time, though, I actually felt elated. Because there was no way Imogene could have heard the rumors yet if she was considering not even coming over.

I gripped the telephone a little tighter. "Look, sweetheart, you won't have to do anything but put your feet up. You can even doze off during dinner if you like, and I won't care. If you're still asleep tomorrow morning, I'll just stick a few flowers in your hair and tell folks you're my centerpiece."

Imogene laughed. Did I mention I was a silver-tongued devil? "OK, Haskell," she said, "you win. I'm on my way."

I think I smiled right up until she drove up my driveway. I kept right on smiling even though I was running around the whole time cleaning, and picking up stuff, and taking out the trash.

Melba says that I have the same interior decorating scheme at home as I do in my office. She refers to my living room as Bermuda Rectangle Number Two, which, I must say, is pretty unkind. I will admit, though, that I do have my share of books and magazines and newspapers scattered all over the place. I use a wooden wire spool turned on its side for a coffee table. This thing comes in right handy because you can get a lot of books and magazines out of sight by stacking them on that bottom rim. I'd gotten all the magazines picked up off the couch and got it to where you could actually see the top of one of my end tables, and I'd put all the glasses and dirty dishes in the dishwasher by the time I heard Imogene coming up the driveway.

Actually, I didn't hear Imogene. What I heard was Rip. I'd just put the last of the glasses in the dishwasher and was wiping down the counter in my kitchen when Rip started carrying on like maybe he thought a couple dozen hit men had showed up. He raced into the living room, barking, and growling, and wriggling all over, in pure canine joy at getting to throw a fit twice in one hour. He seemed to be enjoying himself so much that I just let him carry on—right up until he started throwing himself at the front door.

"No, Rip!" I hated to ruin his fun, but the impact of Rip's body against the door was rattling the windows. "NO! Stop that! NO, Rip! NO! Cut that out!"

Rip, of course, immediately reacted to his master's commands. He howled a little louder. He was backing up, preparing to hurl himself once again at my front door, when I ran over and opened the door.

Rip immediately raced outside. Out on the deck he was a blur of motion, dancing back and forth, and snarling, and barking, and baring his teeth. And, on top of all this, tossing in a few nervous looks toward the garage.

Watching him, I felt like holding up one of those signs judges hold up during Olympic competitions. I'd say, in this instance, I'd give old Rip a 9.2 out of a possible 10. His style wasn't so great, but he sure earned extra points for enthusiasm and degree of difficulty.

Once he was out on the deck, Rip had to recognize Imogene's car heading his way. Imogene's car is pretty distinctive—it's a vintage sixties, bright red Mustang that's been completely restored. In the two years or so that we've been dating, Imogene's distinctive car has been over here more times than I can count, and yet Rip continues to carry on every single time she arrives, as if he'd never seen her car before. Imogene herself has been over here many times in the two years or so that we've been dating, but Rip doesn't recognize her any more than he does her car, or me, for that matter. Now, even after Imogene had gotten out of her car and started up the stairs toward me, Rip still carried on.

I felt a little like carrying on myself. Imogene sure was a sight for sore eyes. She had on a short navy blue wool coat, bright red turtleneck sweater, and faded blue jeans that all but hugged her legs. Her hair was a mass of soft brown curls framing her sweet face, and her skin all but glowed.

I was so glad to see her, I felt like leaping in the air a couple times myself.

Rip, though, beat me to it. Quite a few more times than a couple, too.

Imogene was real good about Rip's antics. She spoke to the dog as if she didn't even notice that he was acting as if he wanted to tear out her throat. "Hey Rip, howyadoing, boy?"

Rip snarled and quivered. And growled and drooled.

Whatta charmer.

I try not to let it bother me that, every time Imogene comes over, she speaks to Rip before she speaks to me. "Oooo, Rip, you're scary," Imogene was now saying. "You're a scary dog. Oh sweetie, I'm just terrified." She spoke in the high-pitched tone adults generally reserve for talking to babies.

When Imogene was almost to the top of the steps, Baby Rip abruptly cut the hysterics and scooted over to the edge. I'm not sure if he was expecting her to pick him up the way I always do at this point, or if he did this just out of habit. He was, of course, totally blocking Imogene's path, but Imogene eased by him, scratching the top of his head in a way that made that dumb dog's eyes roll back in his head.

I stepped forward. "Imogene." That was all I said. And then Imogene kissed me in a way that I believe made my own eyes roll back in my head.

After that, it seemed just like every other evening that Imogene had spent over at my house. Except, of course, that I couldn't recall

my hands ever being so cold or them shaking
quite so much. Imogene didn't seem to notice,
however. She just tossed her coat on the back
of one of the red plaid chairs in my living
room and followed me out to the kitchen, talking up a storm.

While I fixed us a sirloin steak dinner, complete with baked potato and broccoli with
Hollandaise sauce—made from a genuine
mix—Imogene told me what all had gone on
at the realtor's convention in Louisville. It
sounded to me as if it could've been renamed
"Zig Ziglar Sells Houses," but I loved watching
Imogene's sweet face as she talked.

Imogene and I have had something in common from day one: more than our share of
freckles. Fact is, she and I had the same nick-
name in high school—Spatterface. Which goes
to show you just how thoughtful and kind
high school kids can be.

Imogene's eyes were dancing as she went on
about the conference. Her eyes are her best
feature. Fringed in thick, curly lashes, they're
mainly hazel, but they have a definite green
cast. If you look close, you can see that they
have tiny golden flecks in them, too. It's as if
her eyes have little golden freckles, just like
those sprinkling her nose and cheeks.

Rip, of course, did what he always does
when I'm cooking steak. He stared holes
through me, and when I looked his way, he

whimpered. A couple of times, that dumb dog's whimper got so loud, I had to toss him a piece of steak just to shut him up enough so that I could hear Imogene.

Hey, I knew I was only rewarding Rip for bad behavior, but I had too much on my mind already to add dog training to the list. In fact, it seemed like an eternity before dinner was finally over. Adorable woman that she is, Imogene insisted on helping me clear away the dishes, so it was still a little while before she and I were back out in my living room, sitting on my couch. Rip had followed us, of course, and he immediately plopped down at my feet and started taking a quick snooze.

With all this time to get myself ready, you'd think it would've been easy to just turn to Imogene and say, "Sweetheart, I need to talk to you about something." As it was, my mouth had gone so dry, my tongue made little clicking sounds as I spoke.

Imogene must not have had any idea what I was about to say, because she interrupted me. "Oh, Haskell, you know what would be good right now? A chocolate milk shake! Doesn't that sound good? Why don't we just get in the car right this minute and drive to the Dairy Queen in E-town, and get ourselves one, OK? Let's do that, all right?"

I just looked at her. It was February, for God's sake. "It's a little cold for a milk shake, isn't it?" I took another deep breath, and fervently wished for a glass of water. "Look, Imogene, what I'm trying to say here is that—"

I reached for one of her hands, but Imogene immediately pulled away, getting to her feet. "You know, Haskell, you're absolutely right. It is too cold for a milk shake. What would be really good is hot chocolate. Let's go get some, OK? We can go to the Dairy Queen in Elizabethtown, or the McDonald's, or even—" She started to go for her coat. Moving pretty quickly.

"Imogene, wait a minute, OK?" I said. "I'm trying to ask you something—"

She stopped then, took a deep breath, and turned around to face me. "OK, Haskell," she said. Her voice sounded strange. "Have it your way."

With Imogene staring at me like that, arms crossed against her chest, I could feel my heart speeding up. My heart felt, in fact, as if it were going to burst right out of my chest, much like the alien did in the movie by the same name. It didn't help any to have the blood roaring in my ears like some kind of freight train, either.

In spite of an alien heart and freight train ears, I pushed doggedly on. "Imogene, you and I have known each other for an awful long time, and—" Imogene, though, must not have realized where I was going with this because she turned and walked over to the large window to the right of my front door. She just stood there, looking out, her back to me.

I'd been intending to do it up big just like you're supposed to, and get down on bended knee when I did the actual asking. It appeared to me, however, that it would be a tad awkward to get down on bended knee when Imogene wasn't even looking at me. So I scrapped the whole knee idea and went with just going over and standing next to her.

That, of course, put me right by the end table that I keep the garage door opener on. My hands were shaking so much, I was afraid Imogene might think I had some dreaded affliction, like Saint Vitus' dance, and would refuse to marry me for health reasons. So I picked up the garage door opener and started fooling with the thing, just to give my hands something to do besides a damn fine imitation of leaves in the wind.

As Imogene continued to look out at my driveway, I took a deep breath. "Imogene, I love you very much. And what I want to know is—"

She interrupted me. "I love you, too, Haskell," she said, giving me a quick smile. "Boy, it sure is a nice night, isn't it? We ought to go for a drive."

I blinked at that one. Wait a second. Hadn't she said earlier that she didn't want to get into the car again? I didn't give that more than a passing thought, however. I was too intent on getting out what I had to say. "Imogene, what I need to know is—"

I was fooling with the door opener big time now. I could hear the garage door starting to move outside even as I finished saying, "Imogene, will you marry me?"

Her reaction was not quite what I'd hoped it would be.

Imogene screamed.

10

Of all the possible reactions I thought Imogene might have to my proposing marriage, screaming her head off was definitely not one of them.

I couldn't speak for a moment. I just stared at her. Maybe I was just being a tad pessimistic, but I had to admit that this did not look good.

It was just as well that I couldn't speak. Imogene's scream had awakened Rip, and he immediately started howling, looking first at me and then over at Imogene, his eyes wild. Imogene probably would've had a hard time hearing me if I'd opened my mouth. Imogene, in fact, was practically shouting herself when she said, "Haskell, look!" She pointed toward my garage.

Any other time, I probably would've been pretty alarmed to see what she was pointing at, but under the present circumstances, my first reaction was a rush of relief. This certainly explained a lot.

The door to my garage was now down. I must've accidentally pressed the button that closed the door when I was fumbling around with the remote control, trying to keep my hands from shaking.

When the door had been up, it had been out of sight; now, with the door down, I could see what had been painted on its front. Actually, with the garage door closed, you couldn't miss it. Bright red letters always show up real well against a white painted surface. The letters read

MIND YOUR OWN BIZNESS,
OR YOULL DIE 2!

Rip had stopped his howling and had padded over to stand close to me, his body leaning heavily against my legs. I couldn't help but remember how many anxious glances that dumb dog had given the garage since I'd gotten home. Could he have been trying to tell me something?

Wouldn't you know it? The one time Rip might've actually tried to behave like Lassie— doing his best to somehow let me know that, yes, Timmy had indeed fallen in the well, and oh, by the way, some weirdo scribbled on the garage—and I had not understood anything of what he was trying to tell me. I do believe I would've driven Lassie nuts. She'd have been going for my throat by the second episode.

Imogene's eyes were so large, they seemed to fill her face. "Haskell, do you think that's blood?"

I swallowed, staring some more at the message. Those red letters sure did look a lot like blood. In a couple of spots, the writing had started to turn brown. It had run a little in a few places, too, dribbling crimson down the white surface of the garage door. But, let's get real here, that message could not really be written in blood, could it? Those letters were pretty big. It would take an awful lot of blood to write all that. If that red really was blood, whoever had donated to the cause was either quite anemic by now—or no longer among the living.

Which, come to think of it, might've been what the writer was trying to say when he wrote "Youll *die 2.*" So, the question was, did that mean You'll die, *too*? As in *also*? Or was the writer trying to say You'll die *second*?

This is a prime example of why you need to pay attention during high school English—and something, oddly enough, that no teacher ever thinks to tell you. They never mention that you really need to know grammar and spelling so that the next time you're penning a note in blood on somebody's garage, you'll be able to convey precisely what you mean.

If what my garage decorator had meant to

say was *You'll die second*, then that could sure lead you to wonder if there was somebody out there somewhere who had already died first.

Around these parts, it could also lead you to give Sheriff Vergil Minrath a fast phone call. Old Verg was not going to be happy about being phoned at home after hours, but I was pretty sure that if I didn't phone him, he'd be a lot less happy. Vergil takes threatening messages that mention the word *die* pretty seriously. Actually, to be absolutely accurate, Vergil takes threatening messages mentioning the word *die* seriously if they are sent or received in his jurisdiction. Folks living in, oh, say, E-town, or Louisville, for example, could write all the messages in blood that they wanted to, threatening hordes of their neighbors, and I don't believe Vergil would lose a minute's sleep over it.

Before I called him, though, I reckoned I'd better get my facts straight. I was pretty sure Vergil would want to know the answer to Imogene's question. "Imogene," I said, "you wait here. I'm going to take a closer look at that message, and try to figure out what that red stuff is."

I went to the closet, got my leather coat, and when I turned around, I realized that Imogene had apparently not heard what I'd said. She was putting on her own coat, and when I headed out the front door, she—and Rip, of course—followed me right out onto the deck.

Rip stayed with me until I started down the steps. Then, with a little whine, he plopped down at the very edge of the steps and stared after me, his black eyes infinitely sad.

When I ignored him and continued to move down the steps, Rip whined again. A little louder this time. Which was his way of re-minding me—since it had apparently slipped my mind—that he really did need to be *carried* down the stairs. Sometimes, I get the idea that Rip really does believe that I'm not all that bright—and that, poor mental defective that I am, I need constant reminding of my responsi-bilities.

I decided that if Rip wanted to believe I was dumb, it was OK with me. I had more pressing problems to contend with. I ignored Rip's third whine and turned back toward the garage. I ex-pected Imogene to stay up on the deck with Rip, but she kept right on coming. With Rip sit-ting where he was, more or less blocking access to the steps, Imogene had to inch around him.

Rip isn't as dumb as he apparently thinks I am. He immediately caught on that he was about to be left up on the deck all by his lone-some, so this time he didn't just whine, he howled. A long, plaintive sound that made Imo-gene jump.

"Imogene," I said, "you stay on the deck with Rip, and let me check this out."

I was just trying to protect her—if what was

on the garage really was blood, there was no reason she had to see it up close—but Imogene gave me The Look. Every man in America, I do believe, is very familiar with The Look. It's that cold steel expression on a woman's face that says, *Boy, you just stepped in it big time.*

I might've asked Imogene what I'd said to offend her, but Rip was howling a little tune by then. Once again, the only way I could've been heard over Rip's Howling Hit was to yell, and this didn't seem like the kind of conversation you wanted to have at the top of your lungs. Rip, on the other hand, was having himself a high old time. I do believe that dog has the makings of a downright successful musical career.

"Rip! Quiet!" I said.

Rip's only response was to add wriggling to his repertoire. He didn't stop wriggling and howling, in fact, until Imogene went back and picked him up. And started to carry him downstairs.

"No, Imogene!" I said, starting to follow her up the steps. "You shouldn't be lifting Rip. He's too heavy."

That got me The Look again.

I wasn't sure what I was doing wrong all of a sudden, but I decided to do what I'd learned to do back when I was a cop. When you're under fire, take cover. If you can't take cover, get outta there. I turned around so fast, I was probably a blur, and I started heading back down the stairs, moving once again toward the garage and the touching message someone had left me.

It only took one close look and a quick sniff to realize that the letters did indeed seem to be written in blood. I actually shivered when I realized it. Good Lord. I would've bet money that it was red paint. If it hadn't been so cold, the moment I drove up, the smell alone would've told me what it was.

Another hint was the way Rip acted. Right after Imogene put him down at the foot of the stairs, he just stood there for a moment, as if trying to make up his mind what he wanted to do. He didn't seem to be even considering heading toward the side yard like he usually did. Most of the time, of course, Rip doesn't seem to think about anything, but this time he seemed clearly to be considering heading toward the garage door. He took a couple steps toward the garage, then realized he was heading directly for the Door-That's-Alive, and then he backed up, hackles raised, teeth bared, growling under his breath. Apparently, old Rip had decided that the door was now not only alive but wounded. And, therefore, even more likely to attack him.

After he backed up, however, the odor of the blood seemed to overpower his fears. You could tell, just by looking at him, that Rip was trying to decide if maybe this smell meant that there was something edible, like maybe a raw steak, in the garage. And then he started going through the entire routine again, moving toward the garage, realizing that the Living Door was right there, and backing up.

Having watched Rip do this a couple times, I turned toward Imogene. Who was pretty much staring at Rip, too. "It really is blood, I think," I said.

Imogene's eyes widened, and her hand went to her mouth. "Oh my God."

That was pretty much Vergil's reaction, too, a few minutes later on the phone. Only a little louder. And a lot more repetitive.

"OH MY GOD! OH MY GOD! OH MY GOD!"

Vergil's reaction was so loud, in fact, that Rip and Imogene both heard him. They were both standing clear across the room when I told the sheriff about the message left on my garage, but both Rip's and Imogene's heads turned abruptly in my direction the moment Vergil started screaming.

As I mentioned earlier, Vergil and I go way back. He pretty much always reacts to any news I might have to tell him with the kind of warmth and unflagging support that you'd expect from somebody who is practically a second father. "Holy crap!" he yelled. "This sounds bad, Haskell, this sounds really, really bad. Lordy, Lordy, LORDY, what the hell have you gotten yourself into this time?"

"Vergil, I'm just working on a case. That's all. I haven't gotten myself into anything." I sounded like a teenager explaining to his dad why he had not gotten the family car back before curfew. Imogene was standing right there, looking straight at me, too. Which was a tad embarrassing. If I really were a teenager, I believe I would have summed up this entire situation with just one word: *Bummer.*

"A case? What do you mean, a case? What in God's name are you working on this time?"

I should've known Vergil would ask me this. There was no way he would not want to know what might've compelled somebody to decorate my garage, yet I'd told Brother Tallman I'd keep my mouth shut. "That's confidential, Vergil."

"CONFIDENTIAL!" Vergil bellowed. "Somebody is bloodying up your garage, and you say it's confidential! Are you NUTS?"

Vergil yelled this last so loud, Imogene had to have heard it. Clear as a bell. She sort of blinked, and then abruptly decided to leave the room. She walked past me, heading back toward the living room.

"Are you CRAZY?" Vergil went on. "Have you gone BANANAS?"

I decided Vergil's last three questions were rhetorical, and I didn't have to answer them.

Vergil didn't leave me much time to answer

anyway. "It's always something with you!" Vergil was saying. "I reckon all this blood all over everything means somebody has up and died on you again."

Vergil never seems to miss the chance to remind me that ever since I got back into town and opened up my detective agency, several of my cases have ended up being murder investigations. None of them, believe me, has ever been my fault. Some of the victims have not even been clients of mine. Vergil, however, would have you believe that I am the private-eye equivalent of the Bubonic Plague.

I decided I was not going to debate whether or not folks should start avoiding me like the—well, you know. I took a deep breath. "Vergil, there isn't blood all over everything. And I'm not even sure it's human blood. It could be chicken blood, or pig blood, or fish blood, for all I know." I immediately regretted saying this last. Fish blood wasn't all that likely. Mainly because it would've taken a shipload of fish to come up with that much blood. Unless, of course, the fish was Moby Dick.

I also regretted saying it because there was a long silence, and then Vergil drawled, "Yeah. Or maybe it's all them bloods mixed together. Like, in a blender."

Sarcasm can be real ugly.

I cleared my throat. "Vergil, you want to come out and take a look at this?"

I thought there was crackling on the line until I realized it was Vergil clearing his throat, too. "Haskell, Haskell, Haskell." He really did say this. "Every single time you start investigating something, somebody ends up deader than a doornail."

I decided doornails were not a topic I wanted to pursue. "Vergil," I said, "are you coming out or what?"

It took Vergil about thirty minutes to get out to my house. While we waited, hey, it seemed to me to be as good a time as any to get Imogene's answer to my question. Actually, I think it was having blood on my garage that gave me courage. It sort of put the whole thing into perspective. I mean, it wasn't as if I were being shot at or anything. I was just following up on a question I'd asked Imogene earlier. That's all. I was just getting her input.

I headed into the living room. Imogene was standing in front of the large window to the left of my front door, once again looking out toward the garage. I walked over and stood next to her. "So, Imogene," I said. I was amazed. My voice didn't even shake this time. "You've had a little time to think over what I asked you earlier. So, what do you think?"

Imogene turned and gave me The Look again. I stared back at her, a tad surprised. OK, so maybe I'd picked a bad time to follow up. I did know that other folks often had these real cute stories about how they came to be engaged. In fact, I'd heard tell of guys who'd hidden the engagement ring at the bottom of a glass of wine, so that, during dinner at some real fancy restaurant or another, their fiancées-to-be had found the rings right after real romantic toasts. Of course, I'd also heard tell of one fiancée taking a pretty good gulp of the wine and *swallowing* the ring during the toast. Call me oversensitive, but it seemed to me that trotting off to the hospital to have your stomach pumped in order to recover the diamond was a real bad way to start off an engagement.

On the other hand, I also knew a guy back in high school who'd proposed at the top of a Ferris wheel, pretty much promising a real carnival of a marriage. And then, of course, there was that old standby—proposing while standing, hand in hand, looking at the sunset.

I reckon I could've done things a tad more romantic. Imogene probably wouldn't be real anxious to go into her real estate office tomorrow and proudly tell folks that I'd proposed as we were standing, side by side, staring at the bloody handwriting on my garage. Still, I'd gotten this far. I couldn't exactly take it all back and wait for a better time. "So what do you think?"

Imogene turned to look back at the garage.
"I think not."

I blinked. Her answer had been so fast that
for a moment there I wasn't totally sure what
I'd heard. "What?"

Imogene once again didn't miss a beat. "I.
Think. Not." This time she said each word as if
it were a separate sentence.

I blinked again. "You think not? Are you saying that you won't marry me?" I couldn't keep
the surprise out of my voice.

Imogene nodded, her eyes still on the
garage. "That's exactly what I'm saying."

My mouth went dry all over again. "You will
not marry me?"

Imogene shook her head so vehemently, her
curls bounced around her face. "Haskell, that's
what I said. No. I won't marry you." She gave
me one quick glance, and then turned back toward the garage. "Please don't make me say it
again."

It was beginning to look as if being shot at
would've been a better way to spend the
evening. "But, Imogene, I—I don't understand—"

Imogene ran her hand through her hair.
"Haskell, I don't know if I ever want to get
married. I don't think I like the whole concept
of marriage. Fact is, I've always thought marriage was a real good idea for men. And a real
bad idea for women."

"What do you mean?"

Imogene moved away from me then and started to walk aimlessly around my living room, occasionally waving her arms to punctuate what she was saying. "It's not hard to figure out, Haskell. When a man gets married, he gets a lover, a cook, a maid, a laundress, a seamstress, and any number of other job openings pretty much permanently filled. When a woman gets married, she gets a lover. That's it. And a lover is something she's probably already had for a while by the time she finally gets proposed to. So what's she getting? Something she's already got."

I held up my hand. "Now wait a minute, she gets a lot more than that."

Imogene nodded. "Oh, yeah, you're right," she said. "If she's very lucky and pouts a lot, she also gets somebody who'll mow her lawn and take out her trash."

I tried not to notice that as Imogene was walking up and down, she was having to step around a few stacks of magazines, and newspapers, and an empty Domino's Pizza box sticking out from under my end table that I hadn't noticed when I was cleaning up before. "Now, Imogene," I began, "I think you're being a little harsh—"

She went right on as if I hadn't even spoken. "I mean, really, Haskell, if we got married, who do you think will be the one who'll be coming home all the time to carry Rip out to the side yard? Whose little job do you think that would suddenly get to be?"

OK, so now she was making me angry. "Imogene, Rip is my dog, so I do believe that—"

Imogene smiled, but her eyes seemed to be shooting sparks. "Oh sure, you say that now. My ex-boyfriend said that, too. Everything was going to be fifty-fifty. That's what he *said*. But then I moved in with him, and what do you know, everything slowly got to be just exactly the way I'd been afraid it would be. As it turned out, it was just like that joke—he swept me off my feet and then handed me the broom."

I took a deep breath, trying not to get even angrier. "I am not your ex-boyfriend, Imogene. And I can't believe you're turning me down. I thought you loved me." I also couldn't believe I was suddenly feeling so bad when not twelve hours earlier in the day, I'd been sure I didn't want to get married myself. Evidently, there is nothing quite like being turned down flat to make a man get real interested in getting hitched.

Imogene shrugged. "Well, of course I love you, Haskell. What's that got to do with getting married?"

I just looked at her. Hadn't she ever heard the words to that song? Love and marriage go together like a horse and carriage? Hadn't she also heard that women were the ones who were supposed to be dragging the guy to the altar?

I decided that repeating the lyrics of a song was probably not my strongest argument. Neither was telling Imogene that all the other women in Pigeon Fork would probably jump at the chance to get married to the man they loved. Instead, I said, "I love you, too, Imogene. I really do. That's why I'd help you with the house and all. I really would. We could divide up the housework fifty-fifty."

If I'd perhaps picked a bad place to propose, I'd definitely picked a bad place to discuss just how willing I'd be to help out with housework. Standing there in the middle of the Bermuda Rectangle Number Two, you could get the idea that housekeeping was not a major priority with me.

Imogene certainly seemed to have picked up on that nuance. She stood there for a long moment, just looking at me. Then, slowly, her eyes traveled around the room, lingering particularly on the Domino's Pizza box and then returning to my face.

OK, so I had to hand it to her. Imogene's nonverbal communication skills were right on the money.

I took a deep breath and started talking fast. "Imogene, honey, listen to me, I can be a lot cleaner than this, I really can," I said. "If you and I got married, I'd change—"

Imogene didn't let me finish this time either. "Haskell, I don't think people change. They only get more and more like themselves every day of their lives. And this"—she indicated my living room with a sweep of her hand—"this is you. This is who you are."

Now wait a cotton-picking minute. I believe I was getting insulted here. "Imogene, I am *not* a slob." I believe this last would've been more effective if I hadn't sounded quite so much like Richard Nixon when he said, "I am *not* a crook."

Imogene gave me The Look again.

So I did what I believe most men do under such circumstances. I started talking even faster. "Imogene, if you and I got married, I'd be a different man. I'd change. I really would. I'd do my share of the housekeep—"

Imogene interrupted me, folding her arms across her chest. "Did you change when you were married to Claudine?"

I stared back at her, not sure exactly what she was getting at. I'd changed, all right. From happy to unhappy. "What do you mean?"

Imogene shrugged. "Well, did you get a lot neater?"

"Well, no."

"Did you start picking things up all the time?"

"Well, no."

"Did you do half of the housekeeping?"

I hated to admit it. "No, but then, she didn't want me to."

Imogene nodded. "Right, I'm sure she prayed every day that she'd get to do all the housework, and that you'd get to sit around and mess things up."

This was getting ugly. I could not believe that a proposal of marriage would end up in an argument.

"Haskell," Imogene went on, "I don't want to hurt your feelings or anything, but you're a pig."

That one stung. "Imogene, I don't think that there's any reason to be name-calling. I also can't believe that you'd refuse to marry me just because you don't want to do a little work."

I immediately realized that this last comment was ill advised. Little explosions seemed to go off behind Imogene's eyes.

"It's not that I don't want to do a little work," she snapped. "I don't want to be somebody's servant. And that, it appears to me, is what marriage to you would require."

"Imogene—"

She ignored me. "Haskell, listen to me, we have a good relationship the way things are right now. Why do we have to change things? You and I get together, we enjoy each other's company, we go to bed—why, we have all the advantages of marriage and none of the disadvantages. If we get married, all we add is chores. So why on earth would we want to get married?"

"Well, for one thing, the whole town expects us to." As soon as the words were out of my mouth, I couldn't believe I'd said them. The only way I could possibly explain my blurting out such a thing is temporary insanity.

Little explosions went off once again behind Imogene's eyes. Actually, it looked more like tiny atom bombs.

"Yes, I know, Haskell," she said, her voice irritated. "And, I tell you, I don't appreciate one bit your blabbing it all over town that you and I are going to be getting married. Before you'd even asked me! I mean, what colossal nerve!"

I was shaking my head before she even finished. "Oh, no, Imogene, I don't have any nerve. Colossal or otherwise. None whatsoever."

Imogene gave me The Look again.

"I didn't have anything to do with any of it. It was just a rumor that got started," I said.

Imogene managed to give me The Look and roll her eyes this time. It took some doing. "A rumor that got started? Do you really expect me to believe that?"

OK, I was getting mad again. "I only expect you to believe it because it's the truth."

Imogene just confined herself to rolling her eyes this time. "Yeah, right."

"Are you accusing me of lying?"

Imogene took a deep breath. "Well, Haskell, if the shoe—"

I was pretty sure where Imogene was headed with this, so maybe it was a good thing that Rip interrupted us at this point by suddenly starting to bark his head off.

I was so surprised, I jumped. "Rip! Shut up!"

OK, I admit it, I was a tad irritable.

There must've been something in my tone that Rip didn't hear any too often. He actually stopped barking. He sat down on his haunches and gave me a long, searching look. Then he glanced frantically toward the front windows.

After which he ran to the front door and threw himself bodily against it.

It's like I said before. It's this kind of thing that makes a dog owner proud.

11
§

Rip was having the day of his life. He'd not only gotten to bark at me, he'd also gotten to bark at whoever had scribbled on my garage and he'd gotten to bark at Imogene. And now, on top of all that wild and crazy fun, he was enjoying the thrill of barking at whoever was now coming up my driveway.

I was pretty sure it was Vergil.

I don't think Rip, however, much cared who it was. Friend or foe, old Rip was getting ready to have himself a bark-fest. That fool dog had backed up, growling under his breath, and was getting ready to hurl himself at my front door again. Have I mentioned that Rip is about the same size as a German shepherd? And that when he bounces off the door, the front windows rattle so much, I expect any minute for them to shatter in a million pieces?

Before Rip knocked himself unconscious or did permanent damage to the front of my house, I hurried over and opened the door. Rip was so thrilled, he didn't even go outside for a second. Instead, he did this little leap of joy in the air, growled once, and then finally ran outside, his toenails making scratching sounds on the floor as he dug in, trying to get up more speed.

Imogene and I rushed to grab our coats and follow Rip outside. In all honesty, I don't think either one of us was anywhere near as anxious to find out who was coming up my hill as we were to avoid having to continue our little chat. I know I personally would've hurried outside to watch paint dry if it meant I didn't have to hear another word about just exactly how much Imogene did *not* want to marry me.

Our visitor turned out to be Vergil, all right. I immediately recognized the sheriff's official car—a late model Ford painted a medium tan color with dark brown racing stripes along the side and, of course, the word SHERIFF painted on both sides in dark brown capital letters. Underneath the word SHERIFF was an intricately drawn badge in the shape of a star. You can tell Vergil is real proud of his car, it being so official looking and all. He will get his siren going at the drop of a hat, too—I suspect just so folks will turn and look at him driving

by in his official car. I've never had the heart
to tell him that I've heard quite a few high
school kids call it the Copmobile. I also
haven't told him that the tan color the Copmobile is painted is known around Crayton
County as "chicken gravy."

After Vergil parked his chicken gravy Copmobile in front of my garage, he just sat there
for a minute, staring. I reckon he spotted the
message on my garage as soon as he pulled
up, and like one of the religious images that
folks around these parts see every once in a
while in the stressed wood of some barn, or in
a rock formation, or maybe in their breakfast
cereal, the writing on my garage just mesmer-
ized Verg. He didn't move for the longest time.
He just sat there, gawking. When Vergil finally
finished with his sitting and staring, he got
out of the car, shaking his head. Mournfully.
I'm pretty sure that folks who witnessed the
Hindenburg disaster had looked significantly
more upbeat.

What could I say? *Oh, the humanity?* I lifted
my hand in greeting. "Howdy, Vergil," I said. I
tried to sound as if I had folks writing in blood
on my garage all the time, and that my asking
him over to take a look was just routine.

I was standing on my deck, and Vergil was
directly below me. He had to have heard me,
but he didn't answer. He was still wearing his
official sheriff's uniform—shirt and slacks also

in distinctive chicken gravy brown—to coordinate with his official vehicle, I reckon. I was kind of surprised to see old Verg still in uniform, but then, for all I knew, he slept in the thing. Just so he could get up and be official on a moment's notice.

That's dedication for you.

As he came up the stairs, Vergil kept right on shaking his head. I could remember a time when Vergil's hair was a brown so dark, it almost looked black. Nowadays, though, the brown has become salt-and-pepper gray. Vergil runs his hands through it all the time, too, especially when he's thinking. So that most of the time, he's wearing his hair in a style that makes him look like Albert Einstein's long-lost twin. Vergil has got a pretty good sized beer belly hanging over his official sheriff's belt, and I couldn't help but notice that it bounced some as he headed my way.

Rip seemed to notice the bouncing, too. His head started bobbing right along with Vergil's stomach, and his barking got even more high-pitched. Apparently, Rip had decided that Vergil's stomach was some kind of weapon that Vergil was carrying. Of course, as Vergil got closer, Rip started backing up. Oh yeah, that dog was a regular Rin-Tin-Tin all right. What courage. Even though he kept moving backward, away from Vergil, old Rip-Tin-Tin kept right on snarling, and slobbering, and barking. As if maybe if he made enough ruckus, Vergil might not notice that he was already running away.

Whatta dog.

When Vergil was almost to the top, the sheriff seemed to notice Imogene for the first time. "Why, howdy, Imogene!" He had to shout to be heard over Rip, of course. "I reckon I should've known you would be here!" Reddening a little, he added, "And, uh, well, I'm, uh, glad for you two!"

Vergil always sounds just about as cheerful as a funeral director, but this time he managed to sound like a funeral director yelling his head off. At the same time that Vergil was talking, I was pointing my finger at Rip and saying, "NO, Rip! Hush! NO! Quiet! No. NO!" And, finally, "SHUT UP!"

I was yelling all this, at the same time that Vergil was yelling, but wouldn't you know it? Imogene still managed to hear every word that Vergil said. She did a quick intake of breath, threw me one final Look, and headed down the stairs, brushing past Vergil on the way to her car.

Vergil's frown deepened as he watched Imogene open the door of her Mustang and get inside. "Was it something I said?" Vergil asked, glancing over at me.

I immediately shook my head. "Nope," I said. If anything, I was pretty sure it had been

something that *I* had said. Four words, in fact:
1) *will* 2) *you* 3) *marry,* and 4) *me.*

"You sure?" Vergil said. "Because Imogene
took off the second I said a word."

I took a deep breath. "Vergil," I said, "I'm
sure."

Vergil and I must've stood out on my deck
for a good five minutes, watching Imogene go.
Up on this hill, you can see for miles. In particular, you can see the gravel road leading
back here, looking like a gray snake winding
through the trees. In summer, when all the
maple and oak trees around my house are
leafed out, you can't see the road at all. In winter, though, with all the tree branches bare,
you can see every single turn. I didn't even
have to squint to see Imogene's red Mustang,
looking like a Matchbox car in the distance.
She looked to be going about sixty. It's hard to
move that fast down a gravel road, but Imogene was evidently giving it her best shot,
kicking up a cloud of dust, tearing down the
road as if she couldn't get away fast enough.

My throat hurt.

"Damn," Vergil said.

I couldn't have put it better myself.

"I sure wish she hadn't left," Vergil said.

Tell me about it.

Vergil gave a long, elaborate sigh. He does
this a lot. If they ever have a sighing event at
the Crayton County Fair—along with the hog

calling event and the taffy pulling event—I have no doubt that Vergil would win the blue ribbon. And maybe Best of Show.

"I really would've liked to have asked Imogene a few questions." His tone implied that he might never get over the disappointment.

I ignored him. Mainly because Vergil always sounds like this. Even back when I was a kid, and he'd been hanging around with my dad, he had always sounded as if he'd just thrown away a winning Kentucky lottery ticket. They hadn't even had the lottery back then, but he had still managed to sound like that. What can I say, the man was clearly ahead of his time. "Vergil," I said, "I don't think Imogene knows anything more than what I know. So I'm probably the only one you need to talk to."

Vergil gave out with another one of his blue-ribbon sighs. "I sure hope she didn't leave on account of me."

I was still staring at the tiny Matchbox Mustang that was Imogene's car, but I turned to look over at Verg. "I try to be real happy for folks, you know, when they decide to get married," Vergil was now saying. He said "when they decide to get married," the same way anybody else might say "when they decide to throw themselves in front of semis on Interstate 65."

I turned to stare at him. I hated to break it to him, but evidently, the rumors of mine and Imogene's impending nuptials were greatly ex-

aggerated. I was not in the mood to correct
Vergil, though. In fact, I wasn't in the mood to
discuss it at all.

"I try to act happy, you know, but it's kinda
hard," Vergil was going on, "after what I went
through and all."

Like I said, Vergil has never exactly been a
happy camper, but I'd say his camping got
considerably less happy after his wife Doris
left him. I think what really hurt Vergil's feelings was that Doris hadn't even had the de-
cency to leave him for another man. She'd just
left, moving into an apartment less than three
miles from the house she'd once shared with
Vergil. After thirty-one years of marriage,
Doris had announced to Vergil one day that he
was "no fun," and she'd been out the door.

Everybody around Pigeon Fork had been surprised—surprised that she'd left, that is. Everybody had already known that Vergil was no fun.

He was certainly no fun while he was talking to me about the message on my garage.
Not that I expected his investigation to be a
real knee-slapper or anything. Vergil, however,
managed to make it a real ordeal. For one
thing, he started off by giving my garage door
another long, hard stare. "So," he said, "now
you're getting your garage written on."

He made it sound like some kind of achieve-
ment.

I just looked at him. Vergil's nose has been a

little out of joint ever since I moved back into town and opened up my private eye business. You could get the idea that he actually believes that we're in some kind of competition—or worse, that I might actually be after his job. I mean, thank you so much, Vergil, but that's the job I left back in Louisville. Without so much as a backward glance. I mean, sure it was entertaining, arresting drunks and breaking up domestic fights, and possibly getting myself shot in the process, but I believe I'll just let Vergil have all that glory.

"In all the years I've been sheriff, nobody has ever written a message in blood on my garage."

After the talk I'd just had with Imogene, I really was fresh out of patience. "Vergil," I said, "I'll go write on your garage, OK? I'll do it right now, if you want. Is a Magic Marker OK, though? Because I really don't have a whole lot of blood on hand right now, and I'm not about to cut myself."

That pretty much changed the subject. Vergil continued to be no fun, of course, by asking me questions again and again that I couldn't answer. Like, "What's this about minding your own business? Whose business have you been sticking your nose into this time?" And, "Who's your client?" And, "What are you working on now?"

My insisting that it was all confidential did not improve Vergil's mood. "I tell you, Haskell, if this turns out to be human blood, I'm going to be back. And I'm going to have me a warrant for your arrest."

"For what?" I said. "I haven't done anything against the law."

Vergil shook his head, his eyes as sad as if he were looking at all the sorrows of the world. "Withholding evidence. Obstructing justice. Contempt. Last time I checked, those kinda things could get a person arrested in this state."

I didn't want to make Vergil even angrier, but it appeared to me that Vergil was overlooking something. "I can't be withholding evidence unless there's been a crime committed."

"You don't call this a crime? You *wanted* somebody to write this crap on your garage?"

I had to admit he had a point.

"And if this is human blood, I'd say there's a crime been committed all right. Or are you trying to get me to believe that somebody robbed a blood bank?"

Once again, he had a point. "Vergil, if that turns out to be human blood, I'll throw confidentiality out the window, OK? I'll tell you everything I know."

Wouldn't you know it? That didn't satisfy old Verg. He just kept on asking me who my client was about every five minutes. While he took notes on everything else I had to tell him. It wasn't all that much, actually. He wanted to know how long the message had been on the door, and I really couldn't be sure. The garage door had been up for a while, so it could've been there yesterday for all I knew.

Finally, as Vergil was scraping some of the blood off the door into a small plastic bag, he said, "This is only the beginning, you know."

I just looked at him. "Only the beginning?" I glanced at the bag. "How much are you planning to scrape off?"

Vergil didn't answer right away. He just looked at me, his eyes infinitely sad, for a long moment. "What I meant was," he finally said, enunciating every word, "whoever did this is only just starting, and he ain't in a good mood."

His tone implied that if I hadn't figured this out already, I could possibly have the brains of a chicken.

I just stared right back at him. He thought *I* was stupid, and yet, his big deduction from all this was that my message-writer could be a little miffed? "Really," I said. "You think he's angry, huh?"

Vergil gave me a level look and returned to his scraping. "You better be watching your back, Haskell," he said. "That's all I'm saying. You better be damn careful."

I'm not sure what he expected me to say to that one. *Thanks for the safety tip?* Instead, I said, "Will you let me know right away if this is human blood?"

Vergil gave me another level look. "You want

to know right away if it's blender blood?" For a split second there, I thought the man might actually smile.

I didn't even try to smile at him. "Will you let me know pretty quick either way?"

Vergil shrugged. "Reckon," he drawled. *Reckon* in this instance is Pigeon Forkese for *OK*.

Verg finished what he was doing and turned to face me. "Can I tell you just one more thing?"

Was there any way to stop him? I was the one who shrugged this time. "What's that, Verg?"

"*Maniacs* write on garages."

The man said this as if it were a time-honored truth. Right up there with A stitch in time saves nine, and A penny saved is a penny earned.

I cleared my throat. "I'll keep that in mind, Vergil."

Vergil ran his hand through his Einstein-look-alike hair. "You better solve this one quick."

Rip had barked himself into exhaustion, and he'd been dozing up on my deck the entire time Vergil was scraping the garage door. When Vergil got into the Copmobile and started the engine, the noise woke Rip. I think that fool dog realized that this might be his last opportunity to do his Cujo impression for an audience other than me, so he flung him-self into it big time. Snarling and drooling and barking and dancing back and forth.

Vergil watched Rip for a long moment and

then glanced over at me as he headed down the driveway. His eyes looked pitying.

I, of course, went inside and phoned Imogene.

I got her answering machine. Which, if we'd lived anywhere else, would've not been as bad. Here in Pigeon Fork, though, answering machines have not quite caught on the way they have everywhere else in America. Folks around these parts just don't cotton to talking to a machine. I tried to have one myself, so that I would not need to give Melba actual money to be rude to anybody who phoned me, but nobody would use the thing. All I got was a lot of hangups and quite a few messages that went something like this: "Hey, Lulabelle, come listen to this! It's one of them newfangled answerin' thingamabobs! Here, I'll dial it again so's you can hear the message—" The next message would be a variation of the first: "Didja hear that, Lulabelle? It's a answerin' thingamabob! Hey, Earl, come listen to this! I'll dial it again so's you can hear the message all over—"

I guess Imogene, being a real estate agent and all, had to have herself an answering machine just in case somebody around these parts might break down and actually make use of the thing. I knew for a fact, though, that she hardly ever checked for messages. She mainly just used the machine to screen calls. Calls like, oh, say, mine, for instance.

Her answering machine was still picking up the next morning. I thought about driving over to her place, but there was no guarantee she'd even answer the door. I stood in my kitchen, Rip at my feet, watching my every move as usual, and I wondered how on earth I was going to fix this one.

Who would've thought that asking somebody to marry you could damage your relationship?

There were things, of course, that I could do to take my mind off how bad everything was between me and Imogene. I could wash my garage door, for one thing. Or I could head out to Burleytown and have me a chat with the folks at the credit union where Bailey Prather used to work.

I wondered if the Burleytown Credit Union knew that Bailey was being dealt his Get Out of Jail Free card today. It might be real interesting to see everybody's reaction to that little bit of news.

It might also be real interesting to see if everybody at the credit union had showed up for work today.

And, if it turned out not to be interesting at all, it didn't much matter. It would still give me something to do besides sitting around wondering if Imogene would ever speak to me again.

12

∾

Burleytown is a little off the beaten track. The Burleytown exit is only about a half hour from the Pigeon Fork exit, if you keep traveling south on I-65, but when you take the exit, you're still not quite in Burleytown yet. You have to wind around this curvy one-lane road for about four miles, then you make an extremely sharp turn to the right, and when you get past the trees lining both sides of the old state road that you're now traveling on, you'll find yourself heading straight into downtown Burleytown.

A little smaller than Pigeon Fork, Burley-town does have one thing that Pigeon Fork does not. A golf course. I'm not kidding. It's not a miniature golf course, either. It's the gen-uine article, with a clubhouse, and acres of rolling greens, and holes all over the place with little flags sticking up out of them. Of course, the clubhouse looks suspiciously like a converted barn, mainly because that is exactly what it is, but I do believe it's the thought that counts. And if the Burleytown Golf Course folks want to think that old weather-beaten barn is a clubhouse, who am I to tell them any different?

The golf course is one of the first things you pass after you get past the trees lining both sides of the road. Out here in the middle of rural America, you'd think there wouldn't be too many folks interested in golfing. For one thing, a lot of folks around these parts are still farming their land. You'd think that the last thing anybody would want to do after spending the day on a tractor, out in a field somewhere, getting burnt to a crisp in the sun, would be to go back out for a long walk in another field under that same sun. Even if the long walk through the field was interrupted every so often by attempts to knock a small white ball into a hole in the ground.

Of course, golf has never been my game. I'm not quite sure what my game is, but I know it's not golf. Golf makes me want to take up whittling—or digging. So that I could either whittle those balls down to half size, or I could enlarge those damn holes.

It looked to me as if the golf course might not have being doing all that well, because the sign I passed at the entrance to the course had been changed since I'd seen it last. While once it had simply read Burleytown Golf Course, it now read Burleytown Golf Course and Tanning Beds.

I kind of hoped that the tanning beds would bring in enough additional revenue to satisfy the owners, because I hated to think what might be added next. Out in this neck of the woods, it gets a little scary the sorts of businesses that folks seem to believe can go under one roof. Like, back in Pigeon Fork, there's an establishment out on Highway 10 with a sign out front that says Stella's Flea Market and Video Rental and Taxidermy and Day Care. I think Stella would've added something else, but she ran out of sign.

Recalling how much money Bailey had stolen from the Burleytown Credit Union, I half expected to find that the credit union itself had added another business under its roof. Matter of fact, I would not have been surprised to find that its sign now read Burleytown Credit Union and Pit Barbeque.

Its loss must've been covered by insurance, however, because the credit union sure didn't look any the worse for wear. Housed in a long, low redbrick building, it reminded me a little of the Pentecostal Church of the Holy Scriptures. Which, when you think about it, makes a whole lot of sense, being as how a lot of folks pretty much worship the almighty dollar.

Helping folks with their money worshipping must've really been paying off, too, because the credit union was furnished in burgundy brocade-covered chairs, mahogany tables, and not one but two burgundy print sofas. There was slate gray plush carpeting on the floor, and the windows had what looked to be brand-new slate gray aluminum miniblinds shielding the interior from the morning sun. Inside, even though it was a bright sunny day and close to noon, it was like walking into a cave, dark and cool.

Unfortunately, the two women standing at the teller windows didn't seem so much cool as cold. Unsmiling, they both eyed me when I walked in. One had a wide red mouth, large blue eyes made to appear even larger by outlining them in what looked to be navy blue pencil, and a bad case of what Melba calls "big hair." Melba with her beehive should talk, but even I would have to admit that this woman's hair was pretty large. Brown and curly, it stood out from her small oval face at least a foot all the way around. To be as kind as I possibly could, I'd have to say that her face looked as if it had been partially swallowed by some big brown furry creature.

The other teller, at the window closest to me when I walked in the door, was a short, plump woman. Either her blond, frizzy hair had had one too many permanents or the woman herself had had one too many shock treatments. One reason that this last possibility occurred to me was the blank, glazed look in the woman's large blue eyes. Of course, she might've had good reason for looking that way. As I approached her window, I noticed that she was counting out pennies and putting them in paper wrappers. She glanced up at me with undisguised irritation at being interrupted and said, "May I help you?" Her tone implied that she sincerely hoped I would say no. I briefly considered going to the next window, but to tell you the truth, that Big Hair scared me a little. I mean, if that Big Hair could swallow its owner's face like that, there was no telling what it could do to me.

"You most certainly can help me," I said cheerily, heading straight for Frizzy Hair's window. I gave her one of my best smiles.

Frizzy did **not** look the least bit inclined to smile back at me.

Burleytown Credit Union may call itself a credit union, but it sure had all the trappings of a bank. It even had family pictures and nameplates at each teller window, much like the Crayton County Federal branch had at the E-town Winn Dixie.

It only took one quick glance at her family photo to realize that Frizzy Hair had come by her frizzy hair quite naturally. The middle-aged woman in the photo, who had to be

Frizzy Hair's mom, looked as if she'd recently undergone shock therapy, too. Another quick glance at her nameplate told me that Frizzy Hair's name was Sara Lee. Oh boy. That one took guts. In fact, I'd say it would take quite a bit of courage for parents whose last name was Lee to call a daughter of theirs Sara. Particularly if there was any tendency toward weight gain in the family. And judging from the photo of Sara Lee with her mom and dad, weight gain wasn't just a tendency in the Lee family. It was a certainty. Staring at the Lee family's round, pudgy faces, I decided that it could very well be that Mama and Papa Lee had named their daughter after the one thing they both held in the highest esteem.

Sara Lee was staring at me with cold impatience now.

"I'm Haskell Blevins," I hurried to say. "I'm a private investigator."

Sara Lee's eyes narrowed. "Hm."

I wasn't sure what she meant by that, but since it did indicate that she was actually listening, I went on. "I need some information on Bailey Prather."

I would not have thought it possible, but Sara Lee's face got even colder. "He doesn't work here anymore." Her tone was clipped.

I nodded, now giving her my best dazzling Blevins smile.

Sara Lee did not look dazzled. "Mr. Prather,"

she went on, "hasn't worked here for a long time."

That probably had a lot to do with his being behind bars clear across the state. That, no doubt, made commuting a real challenge. "I see," I said, continuing to give her my dazzling smile. Was there any possibility she did not know that Bailey had been in Eddyville all this time? No, surely she knew. According to Nameless, three women from this credit union had testified at Prather's trial. The word had to have gotten around that Bailey was headed for what they used to refer to in old gangster movies as "the Big House," didn't it?

"Actually," I went smoothly on, "I know Mr. Prather no longer works here, I just wanted some information about him."

Sara Lee glanced over at Big Hair at the next teller window. Big Hair was so clearly eavesdropping, she was actually leaning in our direction. She stared back at Sara for a moment or so and then shrugged her shoulders. I wasn't exactly sure what kind of exchange was going on here, but when Sara turned back to me, she said, "Oh, all right, what do you want to know?" She sounded resigned.

"Well, I'd like to know how he was to work with, if he seemed dependable, things like that." I also wanted to know exactly how he managed to romance all the women he did, when he seemed to me to have all the charisma of a gnat, but I had little hope of finding that one out. "I'm investigating some problems at a church, and I—"

Sara Lee made a sort of choking noise. "Bailey? At a *church*? That'll be the day."

"Oh? He wasn't the religious type?"

"He was a weasel, that's what he was. Last time I checked, weasels don't go to church."

She had a point. As soon as the words were out of her mouth, however, Sara Lee seemed to regret saying this. She cleared her throat a couple of times, and then said, "Uh, look, I really don't think I can help you. I didn't know him very well. Arlene over there knew him a lot better than I did."

Big Hair shot Sara Lee a look that, if it didn't kill, would at the very least maim. I stepped over to her teller window and smiled. "You knew Bailey Prather, Miss—ah—" I glanced at her nameplate and tried not to look surprised. It said *Mrs.* Arlene Burress. Good Lord. Had Bailey been fooling around with a married woman? "—*Missus* Burress?" I finished. I couldn't help but stare at her family photo. Sure enough, it showed Big Hair, sitting demurely on a sofa with her hands in her lap, next to a boy about ten and a girl about thirteen. In back of Big Hair, a tall, balding, heavyset guy stood, his hands firmly on her shoulders.

Of course, Nameless had simply said that

Bailey had been involved with three women here—he hadn't mentioned which ones. Maybe Mrs. Arlene here had not been one of the lucky three.

Arlene patted at her big hair nervously. "Well, of course, I knew him." Her tone was snippy. "He worked right here, you know. I think everybody at the credit union knew him."

I kept my face perfectly still so she wouldn't have any idea what I was thinking. Which was, of course, *Yeah, but not in the biblical sense, the way three of the women here knew him.*

Arlene seemed to know what I was thinking regardless, because her cheeks pinked up some. I hurried to ask my next question. "How many people work here?"

"Six people in all," she answered. She seemed relieved to talk about something besides Bailey. "Three men and three women."

Once again, I tried to keep my face perfectly still so as not to betray what was going through my mind. Which, of course, this time was, *Only three women? Then Arlene and Sara Lee here had to be two of the women Bailey had romanced.* So Bailey really had been carrying on with Arlene here. Or, rather, *Mrs.* Burress. I don't know why I should be surprised. The man had helped himself to $250,000. Did I really think he'd draw the line at helping himself to someone else's wife?

"So," I said, again giving Arlene my patented dazzling smile, "was Bailey dependable?"

Arlene shrugged again. "Oh, sure, you could depend on him to be a jerk." Unlike Sara Lee, Arlene did not look the least bit regretful at saying such a thing about Bailey.

"You knew him well then?" My smile was beginning to hurt.

Arlene's mouth tightened. "Everybody who worked here knew Bailey Prather well. He was, uh, easy to get to know."

I'll say.

Arlene glanced over at Sara Lee, and a muscle jumped in her jaw. "Of course, Sara Lee knew him better than anybody."

Sara Lee's eyes blazed. "I did not! You knew him better than I did!"

Arlene glared at her. "That's bull, and you know it! You knew him the best of all!"

"I most certainly did not!" Sara Lee was now almost yelling. "You were the one who—"

"Is there a problem?" The voice was cool and controlled. I'd been pretty much concentrating on the Dueling Tellers, my head swiveling back and forth as if I were at a tennis match, but I turned to face the woman who'd spoken.

She had evidently come out of the door on my right. Through the open door, I could see an Oriental carpet on the floor and one corner of a gleaming mahogany desk.

The woman who'd spoken was plump, with wavy gray hair parted on one side and brushed back from her face. Her eyes were almost the exact shade of pale blue as the tailored suit she was wearing. The name tag on her lapel said Margaret Hastings, Vice President, Burleytown Credit Union.

"Oh, no, there's no problem. No problem whatsoever," I said. I introduced myself and then hurried on. "I'm just looking for some information on Bailey Prather."

Margaret had not looked any too friendly when she'd walked up, but when I mentioned Bailey's name, her face looked as if it had suddenly been dipped in concrete. She glanced over at Arlene and Sara Lee, who were still glaring at each other, and then took a deep breath. "I see," she said. "Well, yes, I believe Mr. Prather worked here for almost two years, and no, we would not rehire."

She was giving me an employment verification. I cleared my throat. "So, would that be because he stole a lot of money from your credit union and ended up in prison?"

There was a long pause while all three women just stared at me. Apparently, I had a tad more information than any of them thought I did.

Margaret finally gave her silver head a perfunctory nod. "Yes, I believe that would be exactly why we would not rehire."

It seemed like a pretty good reason.

"So what was Bailey like to work with?"

Margaret's face turned every bit as pink as Arlene's had earlier. You might've thought I'd asked her what Bailey had been like to sleep with. "I really think you have all the information about Mr. Prather that we are at liberty to divulge."

In other words: *Go away, I ain't telling you squat.*

"You know," I hurried on, "he's getting out of prison today."

If I had been trying to get some kind of reaction, I certainly succeeded. All three women did an audible intake of breath. Sara Lee's mouth tightened, Arlene outright frowned, but Margaret actually looked as if she might be trying not to smile. She glanced down at the floor, ran her hand through her silver waves, and then looked back at me. "Thank you for that information," she said. "Now, if you don't mind, I have some correspondence to attend to."

She turned and headed back into her office. I, of course, followed her. I don't know, but it seemed to me that her being the only woman out of three not to look irritated that Bailey was going to be a free man, well, that got my attention. I wanted to know why.

"So, Margaret," I said, "have you talked to Bailey lately?"

Margaret had taken a seat behind her desk, but her silver head jerked up at that one. "Of course not! The man *stole* from us. He—"

I shook my head. "Yeah, well, you don't act like you exactly hate him."

Margaret's clear blue eyes widened. "Well, no, of course not. Bailey is—well, he is—"

I couldn't believe it. As she said his name, her face softened a little. If I didn't know better, I would've thought old Margaret here was still somewhat fond of her former co-worker.

I couldn't help it. "What's his secret, for God's sake? Why do women like this guy so much?"

Margaret looked at me and smiled for the first time. "Mr. Blevins, Bailey is something a woman hardly ever sees anymore."

I blinked. "He is?" I was pretty sure that there were a lot of nondescript guys out there with thinning hair. Hell, I saw them every day.

"He certainly is a rarity these days," Margaret went on. "Bailey Prather is a gentleman."

It could not be as simple as that. "What do you mean, a gentleman? What did he do that made you think he was a gentleman?"

Was I missing something here? Surely, stealing thousands was not what anybody would call gentlemanly behavior.

"Well, let me see," she said. "If Bailey said he'd call you, he called. If you told him something, he remembered what you'd told him. If you needed him to listen, he listened."

I was trying to keep my mouth from dropping open. Could it possibly be that the secret to attracting women could be as simple as this? *Remember stuff? Listen? Do what you say you're going to do?*

She had to be kidding.

"Bailey Prather is a very nice guy," Margaret added.

A very nice guy who'd spent a significant portion of his life behind bars.

So much for niceness.

I thanked Margaret for her time, and I got out of there.

A half hour later, as I walked into Elmo's Drugstore, I was still going over in my mind what Margaret had said. Let me see now. In order to be irresistible to the opposite sex, I should be a good listener. And I should work on my memory so if I said I was going to do something, I didn't forget to do it. And I should be nice.

Not exactly the aphrodisiac I'd had in mind.

I was heading toward Melba's desk to check if she'd taken any messages for me, but Melba must've spotted me when I first walked in the door. She suddenly appeared at my side, rattling several shelves of cosmetics as she thundered by them. "Oh, Haskell, I'm so glad you're back!" she said. "Brother Tallman has been phoning you every half hour. Whatta pain. He's been driving me nuts!"

I refrained from saying the obvious—that she didn't have all that far to drive—and merely asked, "Did he leave a message?"

Melba gave me a look. "Well, of course he did, Haskell. He said for you to call him back." Her tone implied I should've figured out that one for myself. "I guess you oughta phone him pretty soon, too."

I knew somehow that I really did not want to know the answer, but I asked the question anyway. "Why is that?"

Melba shrugged her meaty shoulders. "Well, on account of the way he was carrying on and all. I mean, Haskell, he sounded as if he was bawling. Can you imagine? A grown man blubbering all over the place. Why, it was just ridiculous!"

I just looked at her. I'd seen Brother Tallman tear up during a sermon, or when saying a prayer, but this was the first time I'd heard of him crying outside of church. "Why was the reverend so upset? Did you ask?"

Melba shook her head so vehemently, her beehive wobbled. "Nope, nope, nope," she said, "but, Haskell, when you find out, let me know, OK? I've been thinking about it ever since I hung up, and I can't imagine what on earth could've gotten the reverend so flamboozled."

I blinked at that one. Resisting the impulse to flamboozle Melba a little myself—by reminding her in as loud a tone as I could muster that she was *my* secretary, not the other way around—I hurried over to Melba's desk, grabbed up the phone, and started dialing. Fortunately, I had seen the number so many times on the sides of the church van and Sister Tallman's car that I had no trouble whatsoever remembering it.

Hey, could it be that I had already mastered one of Bailey's secrets?

Unfortunately, there was no answer at the church, so I ended up having to look up Brother Tallman's home number in the phone book. I dialed it as fast as I could, and Brother Tallman grabbed up the phone on the first ring. "Kay Fay?" he said.

I hated to disappoint him. "Nope, Brother Tallman, it's me, Haskell, returning your call."

"Oh God, Haskell," Brother Tallman said. "You've got to get over here right away. Something terrible has happened."

When somebody starts acting real upset around me, I tend to do the exact opposite. I get real calm. I took a long, slow breath, and asked, "OK, Brother Tallman, what terrible thing has happened?"

"Kay Fay has disappeared!"

"Wha-at?" was all I could say.

I was just expressing surprise more than anything, but the reverend seemed to think I didn't quite understand what the word *disappeared* meant. "Haskell," Brother Tallman said, "Sister Tallman has *vanished!*"

Oh, well, that certainly made everything perfectly clear.

13

§

The parish to the Pentecostal Church of the Holy Scriptures is about three miles down the road from the church itself. It's just a small, white frame house with a green-shingled roof, green shutters, and what they used to call back in the fifties a "picture" window. I was never quite sure what picture they were talking about that could possibly fit in this picture window, but the picture Brother Tallman must've had in mind must've been the bumper sticker he'd designed that I mentioned earlier. The good reverend had stuck the thing right smack-dab in the middle of his picture window so that passersby could read I BRAKE FOR SINNERS as they went by the house. I hated to tell Brother Tallman, but in the middle of a window, that sticker didn't make a whole lot of sense. It just made you think that maybe the word *brake* had been misspelled.

Other than the bumper sticker on the window, there was nothing about this house that would make you think that it was connected in any way with a church. There were two other houses identical to this one on either side of the Pentecostal Church parish. This is something I've never understood. Folks move all the way out to the country to get a heaping helping of privacy, you would think, and yet they end up living in a house just like their neighbors', just a stone's throw away. Exactly as they would if they'd been living in a subdivision on the outskirts of Louisville. As my dad used to say, go figure.

Brother Tallman must've been watching for my truck because he came running out the front door as soon as I turned into his driveway.

"Hallelujah, Brother Blevins, hallelujah! Thank God you're here!"

I wasn't sure what to say to that.

Brother Tallman gave me a shaky smile. "I feel better already, just knowing you're on the job. I know you're going to get to the bottom of this, Lord, yes, I just know it!"

I believe I've mentioned how folks seem to expect both ministers and private eyes to work miracles. Apparently, even ministers themselves expect miracles from folks in my profession. I sure wished I shared Brother Tallman's optimism. If Kay Fay had turned up missing, I wasn't real clear on what I was going to be able to do about it. My stomach was starting to hurt.

"I've already called Sheriff Minrath to report Kay Fay missing," Brother Tallman said.

I just looked at him. That seemed to be jumping the gun a little.

The reverend shrugged. "Of course, he said he couldn't list her as officially missing until she'd been gone forty-eight hours, but he did say that he would put out an unofficial word to the law to keep a look out for her. I gave him a description of her car and her license plate number."

It appeared that everything that needed to be done had already been done. I wasn't real sure what was left for me to take care of.

"I also gave the sheriff a description of Goliath. Because, of course, he really did need to know what Goliath looked like," the reverend went on. "Since Kay Fay never went anywhere without him."

I nodded. I'd bet real money that Vergil did not consider searching for missing cats as part of his job description. In fact, I had no doubt that Vergil had not written down so much as a single word describing Goliath.

"Good idea," I said.

I let the reverend hurry me inside. Once you went through the front door, you got a pretty good notion that this place might be a parish of some sort. For one thing, the first thing you saw when you walked in was the picture of Jesus hanging in the hallway, on the wall facing the front door. It was the portrait you see the most around these parts—the golden-haired Jesus with the blue eyes and the pale skin. When I was growing up and going to church with my mom and dad, this particular portrait of Christ was on everything—church bulletins, Sunday school lesson books, even the small envelopes we put our Sunday offering in. Back then it never occurred to me that if Jesus had really looked like this, he would definitely have stuck out in his hometown, being as how Bethlehem had to be pretty much filled with dark-skinned, dark-haired Jewish folks. The Holy Mother would never have had to explain to anybody that Jesus was not Joseph's son. Just one look and they'd have known it.

The problem with this portrait had apparently never occurred to Brother Tallman, however. He must've really thought that maybe Jesus had sat for the portrait personally, because the portrait on the reverend's wall was not only huge, it was also lighted. The portrait actually seemed to glow.

In fact, the entire house seemed to glow. The hardwood floors were so clean, you could see your face in them, the windows were sparkling and streak-free, and as I followed Brother Tallman into his living room, I couldn't see so much as a speck of dust on anything. Apparently, when it came to housekeeping, Sister Tallman was a saint.

I, on the other hand, according to Imogene, was a sinner.

I sank down on an Early American sofa, and I tried not to notice how there were no magazines or newspapers in sight. Or how the rug in front of me had fresh vacuum tracks. Instead, I looked Brother Tallman straight in the eye, and I asked the obvious question. "Exactly how long has Sister Tallman been gone?"

Unlike me, Brother Tallman did not sit down. Instead, he walked over to an end table, picked up a ceramic knickknack that had been sitting on the table, and started to pace, turning the thing over again and again. I stared at the ceramic piece. It was an open Bible, with the words "John 3:16" written on the left-hand page and "The Lord is my Shepherd" written on the right, both in a shaky gold script.

I wondered if this was Kay Fay's handiwork. If so, I wondered how on earth the woman had the time. What with keeping the house spic and span, and working at the church, and all.

"Actually, I'm not sure how long she's been gone," the reverend was saying.

I sat up a little straighter. "You don't know?" I was about to add, *Don't you live here?* But I thought better of it when I noticed how Brother Tallman's nostrils were flaring.

Hey, things were bad enough. I didn't want his nostrils mad at me.

"No, I don't know," Brother Tallman said, his tone a tad touchy. "Kay Fay left early this morning, before I even got up."

"She was gone already? What time did you get up?"

Brother Tallman's nostrils flared again. "About eight."

I ignored his nostrils. "Does Kay Fay do this often?"

Brother Tallman shrugged. "Does she do what often?"

His nostrils were really getting angry. I took a deep breath. "Well, does she just take off like this?"

The good reverend's nostrils looked as if they were about to take flight. "Kay Fay didn't just take off, as you put it. She left to do her rounds. Like usual."

"Her rounds?" Brother Tallman was making his wife sound as if she were a doctor.

He was nodding his dark head. "That's right. She goes round to the food kitchen, visits shut-ins, collects for charity—you know, she does the Lord's work—every single day of her life."

"Was she going to Eddyville today?" I really hated to think what I was thinking. But it did seem to be something of a coincidence that

Bailey was being released today and now, suddenly, Kay Fay was nowhere to be found.

As a former cop, I really didn't believe in coincidences. Ninety-nine times out of a hundred, what started out looking like a coincidence ended up being cold calculation.

Brother Tallman shook his head. "To tell you the truth, I have no idea where Kay Fay was going today. Sister Tallman didn't need me to tell her what needed to be done." He walked over to the end table, put the ceramic Bible back down where he'd gotten it, went over to the coffee table, and picked up another ceramic object. This time it looked like Praying Hands. You see a lot of Praying Hands around this part of the country. These are supposed to represent the praying hands of Jesus, I do believe. According to the ceramic interpretation that Brother Tallman now held, Jesus had apparently worn red fingernail polish.

"Kay Fay listened to a Higher Power, you know," Brother Tallman went on, pointing in my direction with the ceramic Praying Hands. "That good woman did every day what we all need to do, Brother. She listened and she obeyed. She would pray to the Lord, and His will would be made known to her. It's what we all should do, Brother, it's—"

Brother Tallman was gathering steam. I figured that, unless I wanted to listen to the entire sermon, I had best interrupt. Quick. "What time was she supposed to be back?"

Brother Tallman gave me a quick frown. Just to let me know that he didn't appreciate being interrupted mid-sermon, and then he said, "Well, that's just it, Brother Blevins. She always gets back by three-thirty. Always. Without fail. You could set your watch by my Kay Fay." Brother Tallman said this last with a kind of pride. "So," he hurried on, "when she didn't show up and it got to be four o'clock, well, I started making phone calls. Kay Fay hadn't been to any of the places she usually goes."

I held up my hand. It appeared to me that I now needed to make a phone call of my own.

Nameless was, as usual, nothing if not efficient. He listened to my question, took down Brother Tallman's home phone number, and in another five minutes, he was calling me back.

"You may be right," was the first thing Nameless said. "Sister Tallman may have visited Eddyville today."

I cleared my throat. It was kind of hard to talk about all this with Brother Tallman standing right there, listening to my end of the conversation. "What do you mean, may have?"

"What I mean is, it's a definite maybe," Nameless said.

That certainly made things real clear. Nameless was doing me a big favor here, though, so I didn't want to sound impatient. I will admit, however, that I kept my interrogation brief and to the point. "Huh?" I said.

"All I was told was that someone answering Kay Fay's description was there. But whoever it was wasn't there to visit, so she didn't sign in," Nameless said. "She apparently picked up that scumbag Bailey Prather as soon as he walked out the front door, and she drove off with him."

Good Lord, could Bailey have been using Kay Fay all along? Could the man that Margaret described as a "nice guy" have gotten Kay Fay to launder the money he'd taken from the credit union? And now he was ready to get rid of Kay Fay and take off with his ill-gotten gains? If this was the case, things sure didn't look good for Sister Tallman.

Or was it actually possible that, during the time she had been his spiritual advisor, Kay Fay and Prather had actually fallen in love? It certainly wouldn't be the first time that such a thing had happened. Hell, you read about it all the time. Women fell in love with men in prison every day, and then threw their entire previous lives away in order to be with their new love. Could it be that Kay Fay and Prather had run off together just like in some romantic novel?

I stood there, receiver in hand, staring at Brother Tallman. I was pretty sure that Brother Tallman would not consider the idea of Kay Fay and Bailey Prather running off together any too romantic.

I hated to ask Nameless my next question with the reverend listening, but there didn't seem to be any way around it. "Do you know if the woman who picked up Prather was driving a light green Aspire?"

Brother Tallman did a quick intake of breath.

Nameless snorted. At least, I thought that was what that sound was that came exploding over the receiver. "The person I talked to didn't remember the car. He thought it could be blue. Or green. Or tan."

That sure narrowed things down.

I thanked Nameless for his help and got off the phone. It took me a while to tell Brother Tallman everything that Nameless had told me, because the good reverend kept interrupting me with "Oh Lord!" and "Good heavens!" and "Oh my God!"

When I was finally finished, Brother Tallman burst out with, "Oh, Lordy, Brother Blevins, do you think Kay Fay has—has been kidnapped? My God, is that possible?"

I just looked at him. Apparently, it had not occurred to Brother Tallman yet that Kay Fay could've taken off with Prather on her own. I decided it was probably not a good idea to mention this possibility to him.

"Yes, Reverend, Kay Fay could have been kidnapped."

Brother Tallman shook his head. "By that

nice Bailey Prather? Why, Kay Fay had nothing but the nicest things to say about him."

If she'd fallen under his spell like the women at the Burleytown Credit Union, I was not surprised that the things Kay Fay would say about the man would be pretty glowing. Hell, Margaret was still saying nice things about him and the man had stolen her credit union blind.

I tried to calm the reverend down, however. "Now, there's no use jumping to conclusions. It might not have been Kay Fay who picked Prather up. Hey, she might phone any minute now, and say that her car has broken down on the road—"

Brother Tallman was having none of that, however. "Oh, Brother Blevins, if something has happened to my Kay Fay, I don't know what I'm going to do. It's just like the Good Book says, Brother, Kay Fay is bone of my bones, and flesh of my flesh, my life, my very present help in time of trouble—"

I just looked at him. If you didn't know better, you might think that the good reverend was almost enjoying himself, suffering out loud the way he was and all. He was pacing back and forth, clutching those Praying Hands, occasionally using them to point at me. The whole performance sort of reminded me of Rip, carrying on the way he does every time I come home.

Was this a performance, too? Was Brother

Tallman secretly not at all unhappy that Kay Fay was missing? Could it be that he might've done something to his own wife, in order to make everybody think that Kay Fay was the one who'd been laundering church money? And to make it look as if now she had taken off with Bailey?

"Man is not meant to live alone, Brother," the good reverend was intoning. "It's like the Good Book says in Genesis, 'And the Lord God said: "It is not good that the man should be alone; I will make him a help meet for him."'"

I reckon I was not in my best mood when it came to discussing just how much a man needed to have a wife. After my recent conversation with Imogene, I could be a little touchy on the subject. Not to mention, I couldn't help recalling the little scene I'd witnessed with Sister Dank. I know it was real unkind of me and all to bring the subject up, at this particular moment no less, but before I could stop my mouth, it had said, "You know, I saw you and Sister Dank the other night. After I got back from E-town."

Brother Tallman just looked at me. Either he should be up for the Academy Award this year—for best performance by a guy being accused of infidelity—or he had no idea what in the world I was talking about. "Why, Brother Blevins, what do you mean?" His voice had just the right mix of curiosity and indignation.

"I saw you and Sister Dank, and I heard her asking you if Kay Fay suspected."

Brother Tallman looked even more confused. "I don't understand."

I took a deep breath. "Brother Tallman, I heard Sister Dank telling you about how she couldn't resist temptation—"

Brother Tallman's eyes widened. "And you think— You actually believe that— Brother Blevins, I'm a man of God!"

Yeah, well, so was Jimmy Swaggart. And Jim Bakker. And Elmer Gantry. So what exactly was Brother Tallman's point?

Instead of saying all this, though, I just shrugged.

Shrugging evidently wasn't a good idea either, because Brother Tallman looked insulted. "Brother Blevins, I'll have you know Sister Dank and I were talking about you. You and Imogene."

Once again, I came up with the question that has become my hallmark. "Huh?"

Brother Tallman looked irritated. "Sister Dank had just told me how she couldn't resist the temptation to gossip, and how she'd just phoned a few folks to tell them that you were talking to me about getting married."

So it was Sister Dank I had to thank for that little bit of public relations.

"And she wanted to know if Imogene suspected that you were going to ask her to marry her. That's what we were talking about." He lifted his chin and glared at me. "I can't imagine what else you were thinking."

I stared right back at him. I was pretty sure he could imagine, all right. Although he might very well be telling me the absolute truth about Sister Dank and all. On the other hand, Brother Tallman had indeed had quite a while to think up a good cover story.

I wondered which scenario was true.

"I stand corrected," I said immediately. "My mistake."

We might've talked about it some more except the phone rang then, and Brother Tallman all but sprang to answer it. He listened for a moment, and then he turned to face me.

"They've found Kay Fay's car," he said.

His face was ashen.

14
§

There are not many spots around Crayton County where you can just drive right into a river. I've always been of the opinion that this was a real good thing, particularly since Crayton County is what we Kentuckians refer to as a "wet" county—meaning that you can buy liquor around these parts any day of the week, including Sunday. It being difficult to find a place in this county where you could drive your car into water over your head pretty much meant to me that a lot of folks around here who drink a tad too much good Kentucky bourbon and then decide to take a little drive might never find out just how wet a wet county could be.

The spot, however, where Kay Fay's car had gone in was, unfortunately, one of those rare places where the ground just slopes right into the Burley River. The Burley River is the only river that runs through Crayton County, and it pretty much meanders all over, like a happy wanderer with no place in particular to go. At one point the river goes right past several buildings that are landmarks of downtown Pigeon Fork, but mostly it just cuts through woods, and only occasionally through farmland.

The place where Kay Fay's car had been spotted was not the easiest place to get to by automobile, which—as you can imagine—I have also always thought was a good thing. The place was real familiar to me, as I'm pretty sure it was to anybody who'd grown up around these parts and ever wanted to put a boat in the water. It was not exactly a surprise to hear from Brother Tallman that the teenagers who'd spotted the car had walked to the river's edge on foot.

"According to what the sheriff just told me on the phone, this teenage boy and girl were out there, getting ready to start fishing, when they saw the car. Partially submerged. Just floating out there." Brother Tallman sounded stunned.

I stared at him. A teenage boy and girl had gone back into the woods all by their lonesome to *fish*? In *February*? I wasn't about to say anything, but that little story sounded fishy to me. No pun intended, of course. Not that I doubted that the young couple had indeed discovered Kay Fay's car, it just seemed to me that most of the time when a boy and a girl in high school go off together in the woods, fishing is not on the agenda.

I was kind of surprised Brother Tallman didn't pick up on this, being as how he always seemed to be on the lookout for any kind of sin occurring in his vicinity. But, then again, I reckon he did have a lot else on his mind. "Oh God, Haskell," he said suddenly, "this looks bad, doesn't it?"

I really didn't want to think about how bad it looked. In fact, I had every intention of just driving to the river's edge without doing any speculating on what might have occurred in Kay Fay's automobile. I didn't want to start thinking on it until I had to.

"Oh my Lord, yes, it looks real bad," the reverend was going on. I must've looked a tad blank, because he went on and added, "Kay Fay's car being in the river and all."

I would've liked to have said something encouraging, but let's face it, any scenario I could think up that ended with Kay Fay's car floating in the Burley River was not going to be something I wanted to lay out for her husband. The reverend, though, seemed to be expecting an answer. I cleared my throat. "It doesn't look good."

I pride myself on being a master of understatement.

Having adequately discussed just how bad this situation appeared, the reverend and I piled into my truck, and I drove as fast as I could to where Kay Fay's car had been found. Unfortunately, even my trusty four-wheel drive Ford was slowed down some by the condition of the gravel road leading to the clearing where the Aspire had gone in.

Not that the condition of the road was any surprise. Ever since they built the state road through here, the gravel road that branched off of State Road 70 wasn't used much anymore. It sure looked it, too. There were tree limbs hanging right down into the road that you had to dodge, and there were huge ruts that you had to try to drive around. Half the time, there was no way to avoid them. You just had to bounce over the damn things until your back teeth rattled. Of course, it helped to clench your teeth every time your tires threw up rocks, sending them pinging off the sides of your truck and no doubt leaving distinctive nicks and gouges in what had once been a very nice paint job. Yessirree, that teeth-clenching really helped cut down on the back-teeth rattling.

By the time Brother Tallman and I finally pulled into the clearing, I reckon I'd clenched and rattled up a storm. As I put my truck in park, they were just pulling Kay Fay's light green Aspire out of the water. That is, one of the Gunterman twins was pulling it out. I've never been able to tell Vergil's twin deputies apart, but either Jeb or Fred was sitting there, big as anything, on a bright green John Deere

tractor, his beefy face looking even scarier as
he squinted and frowned in sheer concentra-
tion. To my way of thinking, there didn't seem
to be a whole lot to concentrate on. A chain
had been attached to the rear end of Kay Fay's
Aspire, and the tractor's tires were spinning in
the mud by the edge of the river as the small
pale green car was being dragged slowly onto
dry ground.

As bad as the road leading back here was, I
was a little surprised that Kay Fay's Aspire had
even made it. Of course, not caring a whole lot
whether or not your vehicle was in good condition once it got to the river's edge probably
made the trip go a lot faster.

Retrieving Kay Fay's car had attracted
quite a crowd. There must've been twenty
people or so standing at the edge of the
water, gawking. I realize that twenty people
anywhere else in America might not consti-
tute a crowd, but here in Pigeon Fork, it was
a mob scene.

Mob scene or not, as soon as Brother Tallman and I got out of my truck, I spotted Vergil
right away. The sheriff was standing as close
to the water as he could without getting his
highly polished shoes wet, and he was looking
as somber as I've ever seen him. He was not
only looking somber, he was looking a little
alarmed as he shouted directions at the deputy
on the tractor. "No, NO, turn the wheel, turn

it, turn it, TURN IT! No, no, no, NO! Brake! BRAKE!"

Either Jeb or Fred kept right on frowning and squinting as he tried to figure out exactly what Vergil's yelled instructions meant. The other Gunterman brother was standing at the water's edge, right next to Vergil, and he was apparently contributing to the success of the entire project by nodding and pointing. Whenever Vergil shouted directions, the twin not on the tractor first nodded and then pointed at the twin who was.

No doubt, for emphasis.

The twin on the tractor seemed to be badly in need of direction, because evidently the soil at the water's edge was plenty soft. If Jeb or Fred gave the tractor too much gas, the thing's wheels didn't do anything but dig a couple of ruts. If he turned the wheel too sharply, the whole thing started looking as if it was about to tip over.

Brother Tallman let out a little moan when we got to the edge of the river. "Oh dear God in heaven, look at Kay Fay's car!" Brother Tallman's eyes were filling with tears. "Just look!"

I looked. It was starting to get dark by then, but you could still plainly see that Kay Fay's Aspire was, to put it kindly, a mess. It looked as if maybe somebody had just driven it as far into the water as it would go, and then simply let it sink.

Only it hadn't sunk quite all the way. It had gone in front first and sunk up to the handles of the back passenger doors. At least, that's where the line of silt and mud seemed to stop. I stared at the thing, wondering if whoever had driven the car into the water had stuck around long enough to know that it had not sunk all the way.

The two front windows of the Aspire were open, which was probably why that end seemed to have sunk faster. The more the car moved toward us, creaking and groaning on the chain, the more water poured out of it. River water gushed in streams out the bottom of all four doors and from under the trunk and the front end.

The windshield, the back window, and the two side windows of the back doors were so coated in mud and silt, it was impossible to get a good view inside. I reckon, as we all stared at the car, that everybody standing there on the riverbank was all thinking the same thing. However, it was the Gunterman twin who'd been doing the nodding and pointing who thoughtfully put it into words. "Uh, gosh," he said, "do ya think Sister Tallman's in there? Do ya think she's, uh, maybe in the trunk or in the—?"

Vergil glanced over at Brother Tallman and then shot the twin a look that caused the twin to close his mouth so quickly, it sounded a little like a trap snapping shut. Which, come to think of it, is probably how we first came by the expression *Keep your trap shut.* Jeb or Fred's trap was shut to the max. The huge deputy actually seemed to be pressing his lips together some, as he studiously avoided looking over at Vergil a second time.

Vergil's look was a little late, though, because as soon as Jeb or Fred spoke, Brother Tallman let out a wail that caused everybody near him to jump—including me. The reverend had been just standing by my side, staring out at the car moving out of the water, but now he dropped to his knees, looked toward the heavens, and started sobbing. "Oh Lord help me in my time of sorrow!" Brother Tallman wailed. "Help me, Your servant, in my time of despair! Yea, though I walk through the Valley of the Shadow of Death, Lord help me!"

It seemed to me that Brother Tallman was pretty much concentrating on his own problems and totally overlooking the fact that, of the two of them, Sister Tallman seemed to need prayers right now a lot more than he did. And if anybody was doing any walking through the Valley of the Shadow of Death, it was clearly not the good reverend.

It also seemed to me that Brother Tallman really should've reconsidered the whole dropping-to-your knees bit, being as how he'd landed on a particularly soft section of ground at the edge of the water right next to me. Stuck in about two inches of dark, gluelike mud, the reverend looked like maybe he was doing his own personal interpretation of a philodendron. Unlike a philodendron, however, the reverend spattered my jeans with several dark brown globs of mud when he hit the ground.

In front of all these folks, though, it seemed real callous to mention this last to the reverend. I mean, the man might very well have lost his wife, and I was going to come down on him for muddying up my jeans? Talk about concentrating on your own problems and pretty much ignoring somebody else's. I did, however, take a couple steps away from the good reverend, just in case he got it into his head to get up and do some more knee-dropping.

Brother Tallman's knee-dropping and jeans-splattering had grabbed just about all of my attention, or else I think I would've noticed the movement inside Kay Fay's car sooner. As it was, I was staring at Brother Tallman and pretty much deciding that, as dark as that mud was, it was a very good thing that he was wearing his usual black outfit—and a very bad thing that I was wearing my usual faded light blue jeans—when several folks in the crowd started saying, "Oh God, what's that?" and "Did you see that?" and "What could that be?"

If all that had not caught my interest, the noise made by the Gunterman twin not on the tractor would have. He still had his lips pressed firmly together, so all he did was make a sound not unlike that of a bull elephant.

I looked first at the Gunterman twin, and then I followed the direction in which his tiny eyes seemed to be staring.

Sure enough, something white did appear to be moving inside Kay Fay's car. When it jumped on the top of the front seat, stuck out its head through the open window, and let out a plaintive meow, there was not the slightest doubt what it was.

"Goliath!" Brother Tallman yelled. "Oh thank the Lord, Goliath is saved! He's *saved*, Brother! Thank the dear Lord!"

I don't know. Call me a doubting Thomas, but wasn't this the same guy who'd referred to the cat in my presence as "that dumb animal"? Up to this point, in fact, I had been under the impression that if Brother Tallman never heard Goliath meow again, it would be too soon.

"Thank you Jesus!" Brother Tallman was still going on. "Thank you, thank you, thank you dear Lord for sparing Goliath!"

Hey, if I didn't know better, I might've actually thought Brother Tallman adored that damn cat. I especially would have gotten that idea when he began to weep loudly right after Vergil reached through the open front window of the Aspire, grabbed the cat by the scruff of its neck, and pulled it through the driver's side front window. Goliath apparently was taken by surprise. He let out a startled squeak and then contented himself with trying to squirm out of Vergil's arms.

Vergil did not look amused. Goliath apparently weighed considerably more than even Vergil had expected. The sheriff also had to hold the wriggling cat with both hands, grasping it by the back of the neck, so as not to have Goliath claw him to ribbons. Vergil was breathing pretty heavily by the time he walked over to Brother Tallman and thrust Goliath into the reverend's arms.

"Oh thank you, Brother Minrath, thank you!" Brother Tallman said as he took the cat. "Thank the Lord in Heaven that Goliath is all right!" Goliath must've doubted Brother Tallman's sincerity every bit as much as I did, because the cat kept right on struggling to get away, much as it had done in Vergil's arms. Brother Tallman had to give Goliath a sharp tap on the forehead to get him to stop it. Even then the cat didn't calm down immediately. It let out one last meow that sounded to me as if it could be calling Brother Tallman ugly names in cat-speak.

Having gotten rid of Goliath, Vergil hurried back to the Aspire. He took his time checking it over inside, and then he moved to the driver's side of the front seat. Reaching under the seat, he must have pulled the latch that released the hood of the trunk, because the hood suddenly sprang open.

I could've been imagining things, I reckon, but it sure seemed to me as if every single person standing there at the edge of the river held his collective breath and leaned toward the sheriff as he lifted the hood of the trunk.

I myself took a couple steps toward Vergil and strained to see what was inside.

I found myself staring at a spare tire, a tire iron, and some rags tossed into one corner of the trunk.

Other than that, the trunk was empty.

Brother Tallman ruined his impression of a philodendron by getting up and following me over to take a look over my shoulder.

Having seen that there really was nothing to see in the trunk, I stepped quietly away from Vergil so that I could take a good look inside the car itself.

The interior was a conglomeration of mud and twigs and general debris from the river. It not only looked pretty awful, it smelled much worse—mostly like raw fish, left too long out on the kitchen counter. The floor mats in the back and the front were covered in so much silt that they looked as if the dark brown mud had been painted on.

I looked over at Vergil. He met my gaze with a look so grim, I knew right away what he was thinking.

Somebody had died in this car.

The body must've floated out the window. Or else, it had been shoved out the door.

Vergil looked as if he was about to say something to me, but his attention was diverted by the way the tractor was now tipping precariously to one side. "OHMYGOD!" Vergil yelled. He ran toward the front of the tractor, waving his arms wildly. "TURN THE WHEEL, FOR GOD'S SAKES, TURN IT, TURN IT, TURN IT!"

I can't say I was real upset at seeing Vergil go. It gave me a chance to have myself a little look-see without the sheriff hanging all over me.

While Vergil seemed to be occupied, I squatted and looked underneath the little Aspire. I wasn't sure what I was looking for exactly. I reckon I was just looking. What I found myself looking at was a few bent, brown stems and narrow, long leaves hanging off the underside of the back bumper. I stared at the stems and leaves for a little while, trying to figure out what kind of plants those things had been. It was pretty hard to tell, being as how they were broken, and bent, and pretty thoroughly soaked.

When I stood up, I took a quick look around. There was no one standing near me. Vergil was still pretty much occupied. Actually, what Vergil was still doing was yelling at the top of his lungs, because either Jeb or Fred was getting awful close to turning the tractor over. "BRAKE! Brake for God's sake. NOW! NOW!"

While everyone's attention seemed to be pretty much focused on Vergil's screaming, I went around to the passenger side of the Aspire, reached through the open window, and opened the glove compartment. It took some doing to get the thing open, and when I finally did, there was nothing inside that seemed even slightly out of the ordinary. Just the owner's manual, brown edged and soaked so that the pages were sticking together. And a scraper and some gloves and few copies of invoices for repairs.

I was kind of amazed at how much space Sister Tallman had in her glove compartment. Hers wasn't any bigger than mine, and yet it still had quite a bit of room. In fact, the stuff in there looked kind of mashed down, as if there had been something kind of heavy resting right on top.

I wondered what it had been.

If this had been Claudzilla's car, I'd have known without thinking twice that the heavy thing had to have been her makeup bag. War paint, I believe, is what I used to call it. As I recall, Claudzilla had not been amused.

Vergil was still yelling at the twin tractor driver. "No, back up. Back UP! BACK UP, you—!" The sheriff obviously left off a word in that last sentence, but I believe everybody who heard him—except, of course, the twins—

could fill in the blank. *Moron*, of course, would've been my first choice.

I knew without even thinking about it why Vergil had abruptly ended his last sentence, though. It was pretty much common knowledge around town that it was never a good idea to call either Gunterman names. It's just like shooting them. It wouldn't do any good, and it would make them real mad.

The tractor twin was headed for the water again, as the tires of the tractor appeared to be digging something not unlike the Panama Canal in the soft soil next to the river. While Vergil's eyes bulged and he continued to bellow, "Stop, stop, stop, stop, STOP!!" I looked into the backseat of the Aspire.

The floor mat was matted with mud, but I lifted it by a corner and looked underneath. To this day I'm not sure why I did this. I guess I was just checking everything out. Just getting a lay of the land. Underneath the mat, the floor of the car was not in all that bad condition. In the rectangle shape left after the mat was lifted, you could still see, for example, that the color of the car's carpet was green.

You could also see a small plastic tube, lying in the left-hand corner of the rectangle. It had been covered by the floor mat. I didn't touch the tube, I just bent down for a better look. Son-of-a-gun. It was lipstick. A Max Factor lipstick in a shade called Pink Passion.

I stared at that lipstick for what seemed like a long time. Until I noticed that Vergil's screaming had started to die down some. Then I went over and sat down next to Brother Tallman. He'd moved a few steps away, and he was now sitting on a large flat rock, holding Goliath on his lap. "She's dead, you know," was the first thing he said to me.

I shook my head. "Now, don't be talking like that," I said. "Kay Fay may still be—"

Brother Tallman's nostrils disagreed with me. "Oh no," he said, "she would never have left Goliath behind. She adored this cat." His voice broke. "She has to be dead."

I had to admit that was a powerful argument. "There's no reason to think the worst," I lied.

Brother Tallman just looked at me. "My Kay Fay is gone, I know it. I'm never going to get her back. And—and she was such a wonderful woman."

I couldn't argue with that. I nodded.

"She was so kind!"

I nodded again.

"She was so beautiful!"

That one brought me up short. We were talking about Sister Tallman, right? Kay Fay Tallman of the long hair, the no makeup, and the exceedingly thin lips? If this was a beautiful woman, I was Mel Gibson. And yet, you don't exactly want to tell a bereaved husband that the wife he is mourning could possibly have barked at passing cars.

"She had so many things she wanted to do," Brother Tallman was going on. "And now, she'll never get to do them. She'd never even seen the ocean, you know. She'd lived her entire life right here in Kentucky."

I wasn't sure what to say to that. Yes, well, there aren't too many oceans in Kentucky. He was right about that. I decided I probably did not need to point this out to him.

"She told me the one thing she wanted to do before she died was to see the ocean, and now—" Brother Tallman's voice quavered, and tears welled in his eyes.

I never know what to say during times like these. I'm particularly bad with men. With women, you can always give them a shoulder to cry on, and maybe a hug, but I wasn't about to put my arms around Brother Tallman. My luck, he'd decide I was making some kind of advance, and he'd be sending people out to get me every Sunday and drag me bodily to church.

Then again, I wasn't real sure just how sympathetic I was feeling for the reverend. I know, I know, that sounds bad. But, to be honest, I wasn't real sure that what I was hearing was really what was so. Like, for instance, was it possible that Brother Tallman really wasn't quite as grief-stricken as he would have everybody believe? Could he have planned this whole thing just to get rid of his thin-lipped wife so that he would be free to be with Sister Dank?

"Brother Tallman, is Kay Fay the only person who drives this car?"

Brother Tallman had taken out a handkerchief and was dabbing at his eyes, but he nodded.

"Does she ever have passengers?"

Brother Tallman shrugged. "None that I know of. Except, of course, occasionally Sister Dank would ride along with her. When they did their church visiting, and all. But mostly Kay Fay drove by herself . . ." His voice sort of trailed off.

I just looked at him. In my mind's eye, I could still see that little tube of lipstick. I didn't want to be thinking what I was thinking. But it seemed to me that there was one way I might be able to check it out.

15
§

To get to the closest airport to Pigeon Fork, you follow Interstate 65 north toward Louisville for about an hour. Then you start following the green highway signs that say Airport until you get dizzy going around curves. When you begin to feel as if you might actually throw up if you go around one more god-awful curve, you'll spot a bunch of buildings directly up ahead with red curved roofs, stone walls, and a sort of Spanish air about them. The airport has recently expanded, adding a parking garage and these strange buildings that look a little like haciendas. I have no doubt that these new buildings are the latest thing in architectural design. They do look right nice and all, particularly in the sparkling lights from the expressway, but I reckon, being a hick from a small town and all, I just don't have the savvy to appreciate them. I've only been to the airport a few times since the new construction, and I just can't help it. Every time I see these buildings, I always think the same thing. It looks like the place should be called Taco Airport.

What the place is called is Louisville International Airport. Although, from what I hear, it isn't all that international. I believe I read somewhere that the only international flights that leave directly from this airport are those flown by United Parcel Service. So, unless you can cram yourself into a carton of some kind, the chances of your getting a flight to Europe out of Louisville are pretty much nil. On the other hand, this could be a very good way to spot international travelers at the Louisville International Airport. They're the folks wrapped in brown paper and tied up with string.

It not being all that international is probably one of the reasons why everybody in Louisville except newscasters still calls the airport Standiford Field. Which is what the place was known as right up until the day UPS began doing flights across the ocean out of the thing. Then, of course, whoever makes these kinds of decisions up and decided that the airport had to have the word *international* in its name. In the interest of honesty, I believe the name really ought to indicate that we're only talking boxes here, but nobody but me seems to be bothered

by this. I reckon it would be a pretty hard sell
to talk the powers-that-be into calling this place
the Louisville International *Package* Airport. Although it would be a lot less pretentious.

Louisville Not-All-That-International Airport
is also not all that big. Still, it took me a while
to decide exactly where I should sit during my
little stay at the place. I wanted to make sure I
could get a good look at every single person
getting on a plane.

I thought at first the best place to do this
would be at one of the tables nearest the exit
in a bar called the Tobacco Leaf Lounge. Oh
yes, apparently here in Louisville, in case folks
have forgotten that one of Kentucky's largest
cash crops is a plant that goes into a product
that surgeon generals are warning folks about,
there's a bar in the main airport that can serve
as a little reminder the second they step off a
plane.

Unfortunately, there are sections of the escalator leading from the parking garage that you
cannot see from the Tobacco Leaf Lounge,
being as how they are blocked by—you
guessed it—huge leaves. These leaves do not
belong to tobacco plants, oddly enough, but
huge potted rubber plants lined up across the
front of the restaurant. There are quite a few
of these plants—enough, I do believe, to possibly qualify as a rain forest.

With the leaves in the way, the Tobacco Leaf

268   TAYLOR MCCAFFERTY

Lounge was out. So was a restaurant called Kentucky Buffet. In this last, a wall blocked the view of the escalator. The long row of seats across from the ticket counters was pretty much out because tickets can be checked outside the building.

Through the process of elimination, I finally came to the conclusion that there really was only one spot in the airport where you could get a good look at every single person getting onto a plane. That spot would be on the main floor, in front of the clear Plexiglas half wall overlooking the escalators. You can't miss this particular set of escalators, because they run directly beneath the enormous wire horse sculpture suspended from the ceiling. Actually, according to the writing on the clear Plexiglas plaque that you can read while you're standing there admiring the thing, the wire sculpture was not just any old horse, but a Pegasus—a huge wire horse with huge wire wings, which is the symbol of the Kentucky Derby Festival.

I'm not kidding. The folks at the airport apparently believe that, in addition to being reminded that Kentucky grows tobacco, folks coming into Louisville also need to be reminded that this city happens to be the home of the Kentucky Derby—a fact which, in my experience, is just about the only thing folks from out of state always do seem to know about this city. Be that as it may, the folks at

Standiford Field seem to feel that people traveling through Louisville needed their memories jogged, so they have this huge wire horse with outstretched wire wings flying over the escalators leading to the gates. Once again, I'm probably not the best person to properly appreciate its artistry, but to me, it looks like a big flying horse made out of chicken wire.

I reckon it could be worse. The only other thing that out-of-state folks seem to know about Louisville is that it's got a real fine college basketball team that's won the NCAA tournament a couple times. I probably should be grateful that they don't have a huge wire basketball hanging right next to the horse.

I figured to stand there, staring at that Pegasus for quite some time, days maybe, waiting to see if my hunch was going to fly, much like that winged horse in front of me. As it turned out, though, I only had to stand there for twelve hours and forty-two minutes—not that I was counting, of course. What's more, I almost didn't realize it when my wait was finally over.

I'd just gone over to the Kentucky Buffet to get myself a Coke and a bag of potato chips. It had been a real long night, and I admit, I wasn't in my best mood. I'd gotten tired of standing after, oh, I guess, the first ten minutes, but unfortunately, every chair in the airport seemed to be bolted to the floor. Other than those chairs, of course, that were in

restaurants. I'd actually tried to take one of the
chairs in the Tobacco Leaf Lounge, but a very
large surly cashier had advised me that this
was a bad idea. Looking at his huge biceps
and the way his head looked a size too small
because it was perched on such an enormous
body, I had to agree with him. When I returned the chair, I went over to the counter,
got some napkins, and wiped it off for him.

He did not look touched by my thoughtful-
ness.

After that ugly little scene, I pretty much
made up my mind that I was going to have to
stand. Or squat. Or sit on the floor. The problem was, I quickly found out, if you squatted or
sat for very long, you got to talk to an airport
security guard. I'd told two different guards
that I was waiting for my niece to arrive on an
incoming flight, that I was gainfully employed,
and that, yes, I knew that vagrancy was against
the law, when I decided that maybe squatting
and sitting were bad ideas, too.

After that, I'd spent my time standing on what
had become two very sore feet, and reading
what had become the hated Plexiglas plaque in
front of the wire Pegasus. They had not been totally wasted hours, however. I could now recite
from memory several hundred words entitled
"The Legend, The Sculpture and The Artist,"
and if anybody ever asked me if the Pegasus was
the wonder horse of Greek mythology that had

sprung from the head of the monster Medusa, I'd be able to say, without hesitation, "Yep."

I'd also had the opportunity to pay for a flat Coke and a bag of stale potato chips only slightly more than what I would've paid for a steak and fries with apple pie at Frank's Bar and Grill in Pigeon Fork. A fact which makes you wonder why we have the term *highway robbery*, when it's not on highways where you get robbed blind in this country, it's in airports.

Anyway, I was more or less grumbling to my-self about becoming the latest victim of airport robbery when a woman got off the escalator and started to come toward me, on her way to the check-in station down the hall past me and the gates beyond. She was wearing a long navy blue coat and carrying a gray tweed carry-on bag flung over her right shoulder. Her shoulder-length, blond streaked hair was done in a wind-blown style that reminded me of the Farrah Fawcett haircut so popular back when Farrah was on that old *Charlie's Angels* television show.

Her coat was partially unbuttoned, so that as she walked, it opened to reveal a matching navy blue dress with a skirt so short you couldn't help but notice how shapely her legs looked in navy blue hose and high navy blue heels. After I finished staring at those memo-rable legs, I noticed that this woman looked pretty damn good all over. She might've been wearing a little too much makeup for my

taste—her full mouth was the bright red I usually associate with stop signs—but she was
definitely easy on the eyes. So easy, in fact,
that I kept right on watching her as she started
to go by me.

I would like to say that she looked a tad familiar, but even now, I'm not sure she did. Fact
is, I might not have recognized her at all, she
looked that different. That's the thing about
women—in makeup and with a new hair color
and a new hairstyle, it's just like they're in disguise. I was actually watching this woman, admiring the view, when she must've felt my
glance or something. She turned her pretty
head, saw me, and froze.

For just a split second.

Then she smoothly resumed walking in the
direction she'd been heading.

A split second, though, was all it took. I recognized her the moment her eyes widened.
And I took off after her.

I had to hand it to her. She tried to brazen
it out.

"Kay Fay?" I said when I fell into step beside
her. I might've thought she hadn't even heard
me except that she did this little shudder the
second she heard her name. She didn't even
glance at me, though, she just kept facing
straight ahead, moving steadily toward the
check-in.

"You taking a little trip somewheres?" I said.

"My guess would be that you are headed someplace where there's an ocean."

She gave me a cool stare. "Sir, you seem to have mistaken me for someone else."

I grinned. "Cut the crap, Kay Fay. I know it's you. Now are you coming back with me real nice-like, or is this going to get messy?"

She didn't even miss a step in those high heels of hers. "If you keep bothering me," she said, "I'll have to call a policeman." Her tone was icy.

I grinned even wider. "You do that, Kay Fay. You call a policeman. Right now." I gestured toward the security guard ahead of us, waiting next to the check-in. "Hey, there's one. Let me call him for you—"

I'd say Kay Fay responded to that little suggestion with real warmth. She stopped abruptly, turned and hit me right in the face with her carry-on bag.

And took off running.

I, of course, took off after her. Once my vision cleared.

I wasn't sure what she'd packed in that carry-on, but it had felt like rocks.

As I ran, I could hear the security guard yelling after us. "Hey, you two! Wait up!"

He needed to hold his breath on that one.

You would think a woman who wasn't used to wearing high heels would've been kind of bad at walking in them, let alone running, but Kay Fay must've had more high heel experi-

ence than I'd thought. She moved amazingly
fast directly toward the escalators, leading
down toward the airport parking lot.

I tried to pick up speed. "Hey, Kay Fay!" I
yelled. "Wait up!" I'm ashamed to say I actually yelled this. It worked when I said it just
about as well as it had worked when the security guard had said it moments earlier. "Come
on, Kay Fay! Stop!"

Kay Fay responded warmly to that suggestion, too. "Fuck yourself, Haskell!"

What a mouth for a religious type.

She was all but flying down the escalators,
directly under the flying horse, but in all mod-
esty, I must say that I was gaining on her. I got
on the escalator only a few steps in back of
her, and I think I might've actually caught her
if she hadn't done one tiny, little thing. When I
got close enough to reach out for her, she
turned and threw her carry-on at my head.

Have I mentioned that Kay Fay could possibly have real talent in the throwing department? The woman could've made the major
leagues. Her carry-on bounced off my forehead and nearly knocked me down. It also
snapped my neck back, so that for a second
there, I thought my head might actually de-
tach itself and bounce down the escalator
steps like—you guessed it—a basketball.

I kept right on running, but being pretty
much unconscious for a second there defi-

nitely slowed me down. That, and holding my head, and staggering. I ran past the baggage claim area, directly after Kay Fay. By the time I'd gotten to the parking garage, I could see Kay Fay about thirty cars over, already opening her car door and getting in. She appeared to be driving a beige Toyota Camry that had to be at least ten years old. No doubt bought for the express purpose of being abandoned in an airport parking garage.

I got in my own truck, and I started after her. The parking lot emptied into only one curving lane that eventually opened up into five different lanes that you could get into to pay your parking fee and get out of there. I could see Kay Fay a full five cars ahead of me, in the third lane from the left. I considered just getting out of my truck and running over and grabbing her, but the line she was in was moving pretty fast. By the time I ran over to her, she might've already gone through the gate, and there I'd be, standing there like an idiot without my truck, waving goodbye at her.

I preferred not to give her that kind of laugh.

Of course, Kay Fay probably chuckled a little when she saw that I'd gotten into the lane that was clearly the slowest moving. I always do this. If there is a choice of lanes in the supermarket, or the bank, or any other place, I am uncanny in the way I can always manage to choose the one that will come to a dead stop. Apparently, my lane had stopped because the guy up ahead had decided to argue about what he'd been charged.

As this guy ranted and raved up ahead, I watched Kay Fay pay her attendant and pick up speed, heading out of the parking lot. I also watched her smile and wiggle her fingers at me.

That kind of thing was really uncalled for.

I was considering going up and paying the guy's fees myself when finally he forked over what looked to be a couple dollars and headed on out. That's right. He'd held up a line of ten cars to save maybe a dollar.

It's times like these that I'm glad I don't carry a gun.

By the time I finally paid my fee and went through the gate, Kay Fay's Camry had turned onto I-65 South and was totally out of sight. The lane leading out of the lot and onto I-65 South was so narrow and curving, I almost sailed into the guy next to me trying to negotiate it.

As an ex-cop, I hate to admit it, but I might as well be honest. I gunned it as soon as I got on I-65. Hey, I knew better. High-speed chases almost always end in accidents. I also knew, however, that I couldn't let Kay Fay smile at me like that and get away.

She'd gotten such a good head start on me that I didn't catch up to her until we were almost to Crayton County. I could see her up ahead after only about thirty miles of careening in and out of traffic. Fortunately, there were not too many cars on the road, because Kay Fay had to be going close to one hundred. She kept on going this fast, too, all the way down I-65, past Shepherdsville, past Lebanon Junction, past Elizabethtown. I kept waiting for the local police to pull old Kay Fay over, but wouldn't you know it? What folks said about where was a cop when you needed one turned out to be true.

As an ex-cop, I hated to admit that one, too.

It was just inside the Crayton County line that I finally pulled alongside her. Kay Fay, I was happy to see, did not smile at me this time.

I motioned her to pull over.

The motion that Kay Fay returned was not the least bit Christian.

I pretty much ignored that unchristian gesture and motioned for her to pull over again. I reckon that motioning thing lacks a lot of authority when you're not driving a police car. This time Kay Fay didn't bother to motion back at me. She just swerved toward me. It was so sudden, I almost lost control of my truck, swerving myself to avoid her, and then fighting the wheel to keep from going off the side of the road.

This time Kay Fay smiled again.

It took me a couple minutes to catch up with her again. Once again, I pulled alongside her. Only this time, I swerved toward her.

Kay Fay reacted pretty much the way I had earlier. She swerved to avoid me, and then fought the wheel to keep from going off the side of the road.

The only difference was, Kay Fay lost.

That old Camry went bouncing off the guard-rail, spun around once, and ended up in the middle of the highway, facing the wrong way. This itself wouldn't have been so bad, but apparently, with all that bouncing around, Kay Fay had hit her head on something. The dash-board, the roof of the car, something. It was hard to tell what she'd hit. It was easy to tell, however, that her back tire had blown.

This is the problem with buying used cars. Sometimes, they're just not dependable.

I was over to Kay Fay's car, and pulling her out of it, before Kay Fay had even stopped looking dazed. Of course, she had to try to kick me a couple of times, and of course, I had to use the handcuffs I keep in my glove com-partment for just such an occasion, but once I'd gotten her out of her car, it was pretty much all downhill after that. I drove to a nearby gas station and phoned Vergil.

Even today, I don't know why Kay Fay headed back toward Pigeon Fork. Maybe she was just hoping to get back into familiar terri-tory so that she could lose me easier on some of them winding country roads around town. She might even have had a place in mind.

Whatever she'd been planning, it didn't happen. And I didn't ask about it.

I did talk to her about several other things while I drove her to the sheriff's office. "Kay Fay," I said, "you must've really wanted to get away. To sacrifice your cat and all. You know, Goliath almost died in your car when it went in the river."

"Damn!" Kay Fay said. "That damn cat is still alive? Hell, the only reason I adopted it in the first place was to make people think I had to be dead."

I just looked at her. I've always been of the opinion that anybody who doesn't like animals can't quite be trusted. Kay Fay seemed to be a case in point. "You mean," I said, "you've been planning this for—"

Kay Fay actually smiled. "—for months. Ever since I met that stupid Bailey, and he started trying to make me fall for him so I'd launder his money for him. He thought he was conning me. Well, he was sure wrong, wasn't he?"

She actually sounded a little proud.

"I reckon Bailey is—"

Can you believe, Kay Fay smiled *again*?

She didn't say a word after that, though. Not a word.

I reckon she knew if his body wasn't found, it would be hard to try her for murder. Once Kay Fay was in custody and all, though, I thought I'd tell Vergil my second hunch. Which was where they could find poor Bailey's body.

As it turned out, once again I was right on the money. Poor Bailey was found in that abandoned cornfield I'd passed on my way to Eddyville—the one on that farm for sale.

I don't know how Kay Fay had managed to get Bailey to stop, or how she'd managed to shoot him, but there wasn't a doubt in my mind what it was that had been so heavy in Kay Fay's glove compartment—the thing that had mashed everything down. It had been a gun.

She must've backed her car right off the road, into the cornfield, and just rolled Bailey's body right out the door. So it would be hidden in the long cornstalks that remained. Some of those stalks had stuck in the underside of the bumper, and that's what I had seen when they first pulled the car out of the water.

I figured Kay Fay had picked Bailey up at Eddyville and had not driven far with him before she'd shot him. Or maybe she'd just told him that she'd hidden some of his money in the cornfield. When he'd gotten out of the car, she'd just walked up behind him and pulled the trigger.

According to Vergil, Kay Fay didn't smile at all when he told her that Bailey's body had been found.

Of course, I wasn't smiling either. Poor Bailey may have been a scoundrel, but he didn't deserve to die like that. Not to mention, I sure would've liked to have heard his secret with the ladies. From his own lips.

I still couldn't quite believe it was Be nice.

Not to mention, his secret hadn't quite worked on Kay Fay. Lord. The last thing poor old Bailey must've felt was total surprise.

It was not, however, a total surprise to me that Vergil turned to me right after putting Kay Fay under lock and key and said, "Haskell, I think you ought to be the one to break the news to Brother Tallman. Being as how you're the one who solved this and all."

He made it sound as if telling the reverend was some kind of honor. Like Kay Fay, I didn't smile.

16
§

I told Reverend Tallman myself. It was one of those good news, bad news kind of deals. The good news is your wife isn't dead. The bad news is she's in jail for murder. And, oh yes, by the way, she's the one who's been dressing up like you and making deposits into your church account in Elizabethtown.

Reverend Tallman took it pretty well. He went from "Thank the Lord!" to "Oh Jesus!" in the space of about a minute, but all in all, he stayed pretty calm. He even insisted on leaving right that minute and visiting Kay Fay in the county jail, to "minister to her in her time of need."

I did hear from Vergil that the ministering idea was not met with a lot of enthusiasm on Kay Fay's part. In fact, according to Vergil, who phoned to tell me all about it, Kay Fay's response could be summed up by just three words—which she yelled at the top of her lungs at her husband the second he walked up to her cell—"GO TO HELL!"

Oh, yes, that seemed like a clear indication of a lack of enthusiasm.

It apparently wasn't all that clear to Brother Tallman, though. He not only did not go—to hell or otherwise—but he stayed around for hours, praying up a storm, and blessing Kay Fay, and even singing a few hymns. According to Vergil, Brother Tallman actually seemed to be enjoying himself. It was Vergil's considered opinion, in fact, that even though Brother Tallman did his best to look distraught at the horror of it all, the good reverend was secretly tickled pink to be presented with such a challenge. "It's not every day you get to save the soul of a murderer," Vergil drawled.

I had to agree that accomplishing such a thing would look real impressive on the good reverend's spiritual resumé.

Apparently, Brother Tallman was enjoying himself so much that Vergil finally had to come in and break the news that visiting hours were over. Otherwise, Vergil was pretty sure that Brother Tallman never would have left. He'd have set up permanent residence just outside of Kay Fay's cell, and, no doubt, would have started receiving his mail in care of the sheriff's office.

Kay Fay had three more words to say when

Vergil showed up to tell Brother Tallman to leave. "Praise the Lord!"

Brother Tallman had actually smiled when she said that. "Lord forgive her," he intoned, "because she knoweth not what she does."

It was my considered opinion—and Vergil's, too, I do believe—that Kay Fay did too knoweth. As Vergil put it, "It'll take a miracle for Reverend Tallman to bring that black-hearted woman back into the church."

It was just as well, being as how it was going to be a little difficult for Kay Fay to attend services, what with her permanently residing behind bars and all. I do believe, however, that this would be a case of If Mohammed couldn't come to the mountain, the mountain would come to Mohammed. The good reverend would, no doubt, be more than delighted to bring church services right to Kay Fay's jail cell.

Perhaps two or three times a week.

Remembering poor Bailey, I kind of thought that might be a fitting punishment for old Kay Fay.

I would've talked to Vergil on the phone a little longer except that I realized that I was just procrastinating, putting off doing what I knew had to be done. Oh, yes, I had me a project I had to get cracking on. As soon as I took me a quick nap.

The entire project took me a good part of the next three days.

During that time I tried to phone Imogene again and again, at her apartment and at her office, but every single time I called, she wouldn't come to the phone. Or she would let her answering machine pick up.

Finally, on the third day, I drove over to her real estate office. Her Mustang was parked out front, so I knew she was inside.

She didn't even let me say a word before she was on her feet. "Haskell, I don't think we have anything to say to each other."

"Well, good," I said. "We agree on something. I don't think we have anything to say to each other, either."

She was heading toward the door—no doubt, to open it and unceremoniously show me out—but that last little statement of mine stopped her in her tracks. "What?" she asked, as she turned around to face me.

"I said I don't want to talk to you. All I want is for you to go for a little drive with me, that's all. I won't say a word to you."

Imogene just looked at me, clearly skeptical.

"I promise. I will keep my lip zipped. On my word as a gentleman."

I wasn't sure if it was just to see if I'd keep my promise or if she wanted to prove once and for all that I was definitely *not* a gentleman, but Imogene gave me a long look and then went and got her coat and purse. Without a word, she followed me out to my truck.

True to my word, I didn't utter so much as a peep on the way. I didn't even look at Imogene either. I just kept my eyes on the road ahead and concentrated on my driving.

Of course, I didn't really have to concentrate, being as how I'd driven this particular route so many times, I could've probably driven it in my sleep. When I made the turn onto the gravel road that led back to my house, Imogene spoke for the first time since she'd gotten in my truck. "Are we going to your house? Is that where you're taking me?"

Again, true to my word, I said nothing.

I couldn't decide if the expression on Imogene's face was amused or annoyed. She really couldn't complain, though, being as how I'd warned her from the get-go that I would not be in a conversing mood. Not to mention, there was my reputation as a gentleman at stake.

Imogene just sat there without saying another word until we reached my driveway. I put the truck in low gear and started the steep climb up. I could hear Rip, of course, in the distance, barking his hellos.

He kept it up right up until Imogene and I were out of my truck and heading upstairs. Imogene, as usual, stopped to pet Rip, crooning to him and scratching him between the ears, until his eyes rolled back in his head.

I think it was on account of her petting Rip and all that she didn't notice anything right away. I stepped past her and Rip, and I headed toward the front door, opening it and holding it for her.

Imogene's eyes were still on Rip, who was padding along after her, his own eyes still glazed with adoration, when she went through the front door.

When she turned, though, and took a look at my living room, she actually staggered back a little. "Oh my."

I just stood there, of course, grinning at her. I must say the freshly waxed floor did look right nice, gleaming in the light from the front windows. Which, incidentally, had been Windexed, inside and out. Along with every other window in the house. Even though it was damn cold outside.

My sofa looked pretty damn good, too, being as how it had been cleaned all of three times with upholstery shampoo. And then, of course, the wire spool that I'd been using as a coffee table was gone, replaced by a brand-new oak coffee table. I'd chosen this coffee table just because it had little doors on all four sides, beneath the tabletop. Behind those little doors was enough room for all the magazines and newspapers I'd decided I couldn't part with. The rest, though, were in black plastic bags in back of the garage, waiting for the next garbage pickup.

Imogene's eyes just kept getting bigger and

bigger as I showed her through the rest of the house. Finally, after she'd oohed and ahhed over my new bedspread, and my new mini-blinds, and the gleaming chrome in my bath-rooms, we made our way back into the kitchen.

It looked like it was now or never. I went over to the refrigerator and pulled out what I'd stored inside. Two champagne glasses and an already opened bottle of champagne. I poured two glasses, and then I returned to the refrig-erator for the bouquet of sweetheart roses I'd bought at the florist yesterday. I handed Imo-gene the flowers and the champagne.

"Imogene, I'm doing it right this time. I love you very much. Will you marry me?"

She had taken a sip of her champagne, and she was sniffing her roses appreciatively. She didn't even look up when she answered me. "No, Haskell."

My heart, I think, dropped to my knees. "Wha-a-at?"

"But we could try living together for a while," Imogene went on. "See how it goes—" She was still looking at the flowers.

I shook my head. "I don't want a trial run, Imogene. I love you, I want to be with you for the rest of my life."

Imogene looked up at me then. She put her glass and her flowers down on my counter, and she came over to put her arms around my neck. Have I mentioned that Imogene always smells like flowers herself?

"Haskell," she said, "the best I can do is agree to live with you for now. So we can see what happens. That's all I can do." She took a deep breath, looking into my eyes. I could feel her trembling against me. "I can't believe I'm even saying yes to this."

Like I said at the beginning, sometimes we private eyes are expected to work miracles. The way I looked at it, I had worked one, and I had one to go.

I leaned down to kiss the woman who one day, as God is my witness, will most certainly be Imogene Bievins. My beloved wife. Who sure can kiss.

**Delight in every
romance title from**

MIRANDA JARRETT

Wishing

Moonlight

Under the Boardwalk

Cranberry Point

The Captain's Bride

All available wherever books are sold

*SONNET
BOOKS*

2380

**Visit the
Simon & Schuster Web site:**

www.SimonSays.com

**and sign up for our
mystery e-mail updates!**

Keep up on the latest new releases,
author appearances, news, chats,
special offers, and more!
We'll deliver the information
right to your inbox—
if it's new, you'll know about it.